T0205049

HAUNT

Sweet

HOME

Also by Sarah Pinsker

HAUNT
Sweet
HOME

Sarah Pinsker

TOR PUBLISHING GROUP • NEW YORK

HAUNT SWEET HOME

Copyright © 2024 by Sarah Pinsker

A Tordotcom Book
Published by Tom Doherty Associates / Tor Publishing Group
120 Broadway
New York, NY 10271

www.torpublishinggroup.com

Tor® is a registered trademark of Macmillan Publishing Group, LLC.

The Library of Congress Cataloging-in-Publication Data is available upon request.

ISBN 978-1-250-33026-0 (hardcover)
ISBN 978-1-250-33027-7 (ebook)

Our books may be purchased in bulk for promotional, educational, or business use. Please contact your local bookseller or the Macmillan Corporate and Premium Sales Department at 1-800-221-7945, extension 5442, or by email at MacmillanSpecialMarkets@macmillan.com.

First Edition: 2024

Printed in the United States of America

0 9 8 7 6 5 4 3 2 1

For visionary artists everywhere—
keep doing your thing

HAUNT

Sweet

HOME

TRANSCRIPT
HAUNT SWEET HOME EPISODE 717—ACT V

> JEREMY *(speaking while driving)*

I needed sleep after a hard day of renovations on the Fergusons' new home, but I was still curious about who or what was haunting them. Why not make a late-night visit and see for myself? It was time to check out their library ghost.

Cut to JEREMY knocking on the door of Cleaveland House. MAGGIE and CONOR greet him in over-sized T-shirts and pajama pants.

> JEREMY

Hi, guys! I hope you don't mind me stopping by. I've been dying to meet your library ghost. Well, not dying, hopefully . . . care to introduce me?

> MAGGIE

We can't just make it happen. Come in and sit down and maybe it'll start—

A loud thump comes from somewhere behind her in the house's interior. All three startle.

> CONOR

Or maybe it's really eager to meet you.

The FERGUSONS and JEREMY enter the library and flip the light on. The camera focuses on several leather-bound volumes strewn across the floor,

*some with bindings broken, and loose pages every-
where.*

                    JEREMY
Oh, wow. So, is this what's been happening?

                    MAGGIE
No, the other books were dropped flat. They
weren't damaged.

                    CONOR
Didn't you call it a cull? What difference does
it make if they land in one piece if the point
is to throw them out?

                    MAGGIE
It's our library, not hers! She can make suggestions, but I should get to decide which
books stay or go. If she ruins them first, it's
not much of a choice.

                    JEREMY
Your ghost is a she?

                    MAGGIE
I kind of just assumed. It felt right. She can
correct me if I'm wrong.

A book hits MAGGIE in the head.

Ow!

                    JEREMY
Where did that come from?

CONOR retrieves the book and examines the cover.

                    CONOR
It's called *Good Wives: Image and Reality in
the Lives of Women in Northern New England,
1650–1750.*

                    MAGGIE
That's a good book! It's not even that old. A
really solid piece of scholarship. This can't
be a culling suggestion.

                    JEREMY
Maybe it's a clue to who she is.

                    CONOR
This house isn't anywhere near that old. I—

A falling book hits his shoulder.

Hey!

                    JEREMY
Spirit, if you want to communicate with us,
give us a sign.

A book wings past his cheek and hits a pillar.

                    JEREMY
Not that kind of sign. I was thinking more like
making the lights flicker.

                    CONOR
What did she throw at him?

MAGGIE picks up the book.

                    MAGGIE
Three Men in a Boat. First edition.

                    CONOR
Do you get the feeling she's trying to hurt us,
or just communicate?

        MYSTERIOUS ALTO WOMAN'S VOICE (V.O.)
If I wanted to communicate with you, I'd just
speak.

MAGGIE, JEREMY, and CONOR all startle again.
Cut to JEREMY at hotel, later.

                    JEREMY
In all my years on this show, we'd never en-
countered a haunting with the power of speech.
I was eager to communicate, but cautious about
upsetting the spirit further.

Cut to library interior. MAGGIE has a hand on
the ladder.

                    MAGGIE
I want to see where the books are coming from.

                    JEREMY
Do you think it's smart to go up there? What if
it makes her throw even more books?

                    MAGGIE
I'm gonna risk it.

MAGGIE climbs the library ladder while the others
look on. At the top, she holds the rails and sur-
veys her surroundings.

                    MAGGIE
I don't see anything out of place. Maybe on the
other side?

Somebody screams. Then a second, inhuman scream
fills the room. More books fall. The camera
whirls upward. A black shape flies off the bal-
cony and crashes into JEREMY. Cut to MAGGIE
sliding down the ladder, more books falling
behind her. Cut to the bulbs in the chandelier
exploding, leaving everyone in darkness. The
library door creaks open and the camera whirls
again to capture the black shape racing through
before the door slams shut behind it. Cut to

*everyone looking upward as if waiting for more
falling books.*

                    JEREMY
Wow. In all my time on this show, I have to say
without a doubt that's the eeriest thing I've
ever experienced. How are you two feeling?

                    CONOR
I always thought this show was faked, but that
was the real deal!

                    MAGGIE
There's no other explanation.

I

If Uncle AJ hadn't screwed up Thanksgiving, I would never have learned how to haunt houses.

I pulled up at four sharp, just behind Aunt Bea and just ahead of my parents, my hatchback tiny between their SUVs. We parked on the lawn, since the driveway was already full; we're a punctual family. I recognized all the vehicles except a spotless new Rivian, which had to mean my cousin Jeremy had decided to grace us with his presence. He came in for a holiday every few years so everyone could tell him how great he was.

I reached into my backseat for the case of Yuengling I'd bought for the potluck, only to realize I'd forgotten it at my apartment. A bunch of random plastic grocery bags littered the footwell, so I stuffed those into a larger reusable bag to make it look like I was carrying something. Once I got into the house nobody would remember what I'd contributed; I didn't have a signature dish, like Aunt Del's pies or Uncle Gary's green bean casserole.

My parents and I hadn't seen each other for a couple of months, since I'd started working nights, and we exchanged one-armed hugs when we got close enough. Dad carried his fiddle case in his left, and my mother hefted a vat filled with her version of Oma's stuffing, but even without our hands full, we're a one-armed-hug family.

The brick path had sunken in various spots, and now those spots were filled with icy slush. With my eyes down to avoid wiping out in the dimming light, I didn't notice the bottle-necked crowd gathered on the porch until we'd reached the step below them.

"AJ's not answering," said Aunt Bea. "We've tried the door and his phone. All the lights are off too." She didn't sound overly concerned. His car wasn't there, so he probably wasn't lying dead on the floor inside.

She turned to me. "Mara, you didn't see him down at the apartments, did you?"

I'd been living at his little six-unit rental property for a few years now. Reduced rent in exchange for mowing the lawn and doing light maintenance and letting my neighbors in when they locked themselves out. I shook my head; he hadn't come around in weeks.

Aunt Del gestured in the direction of my grandmother's house on the other side of the tree line. "Gary's picking up Mom on his way, so we told him to grab AJ's spare key while he was there."

Everyone stood around pretending their Tupperware and casseroles and Crock-Pots weren't getting heavier the longer we waited. Jeremy cradled the biggest bottle of red wine I'd ever seen. My dad asked if it was like those novelty checks they give lottery winners, and Jeremy winesplained to us about bottle sizing and said it was a jeroboam.

"Quantity over quality," someone joked, but Jeremy looked annoyed.

"Trust me," he said. "It's a very nice wine. The production company sent it to celebrate *Haunt Sweet Home*'s renewal. I'm just sharing the love."

To which his own mother replied, "Never too rich to appreciate something free," which might have been either an insult or a compliment, it was impossible to tell.

It was cold enough to see our breath. We all stamped our feet and pretended we weren't chilly, and collectively perked up when headlights bobbed up the rutted drive. Uncle Gary pulled his pickup onto the lawn and all the way to the steps before he hopped out. He ran around to the truck's open bed and grabbed a white plastic stepstool, which he threw in front of the passenger side. Oma opened her door and eyed the dismount. After a pause, she descended carefully, like a queen, resting one twisted hand on Gary's arm and the other on the door.

"I hate this fucking truck," she said. "It's too tall. It's so fancy you're afraid to get it dirty, and it isn't even strong enough to pull a trailer."

"Fair point," someone muttered.

"Why does a dentist need to pull a trailer?" someone else asked.

Gary transferred Oma's hand to the railing before hauling himself up into his truck and pulling away, splattering the lower steps and his mother with mud, possibly to prove a point about getting dirty. He left furrows that AJ was sure to be pissed about, whenever he finally graced us with an appearance. Aunt Del helped Oma up the steps, then Oma fished in her bag and retrieved a house key. The family invaded.

AJ did not seem to have been expecting us. He hadn't replaced the furniture Aunt Carmen had taken when she left; the absences of the coffee table and the hutch full of ceramic dogs were conspicuous, beyond the dents left in the carpet. There was no scent of roasting turkey, just a stale odor like the windows hadn't been opened in a while. Dirty dishes in the sink, dining room table covered in clean laundry ("At least he's doing laundry?" "At least she left the dining room table."), a pillow and blanket nestled in a depression in the couch opposite the TV. I stashed my bag of bags in the pantry next to AJ's bag of bags; it looked right at home.

"Poor AJ," Del said. That and the table comment were the closest anyone got to mentioning the divorce.

Dad propped his fiddle case beside the couch and rolled up his sleeves. "Dish duty for me."

The aunts and uncles and cousins started clearing the laundry and setting up the buffet, while my cousins' children ran through the house with no regard for closed doors. Oma supervised everything from the La-Z-Boy. I leaned against the kitchen wall, still in my puffy jacket, and watched the extended Billings family as they demonstrated their effortless competence, trying to figure out if there was something for me to do or if I should stay out of the way. They always seemed to fit together like a machine when something needed doing; I was just a spare part.

Jeremy appeared from the basement with a dusty-looking six-pack of something I didn't recognize. He put a finger to his lips and motioned his head toward the back door. I grabbed a box of cheese crackers on my way, since there was no telling when we'd actually eat dinner. Nobody else followed, but all the other cousins were involved in the big cleanup.

We stopped at the shed first. Dry firewood was piled along the wall, and the recycling bin was full of burnable supermarket circulars. We each grabbed as much wood and paper as we could carry to the fire pit, another fifty feet back. The thrones were still out, which surprised me; usually they got dragged to the shed before November.

Jeremy dumped his logs beside the pit and draped himself over the official Jeremy chair, the one with the lion's head resting its chin near his left shoulder, its body twined around the back and arms. His was one of only two chairs with arms, since musicians can't play in armchairs; he and Oma weren't musical like everyone else. Well, everybody else but me, but I had no throne of my own.

I took his lounging posture to mean he expected me to build the fire. I made a quick A-frame, then patted my pockets like the kind of person who carried matches.

"Be prepared." Jeremy tossed me his lighter. He'd been an Eagle Scout.

The kindling caught quickly, and I turned away to choose my throne. The second one on Jeremy's left was my father's, with the forested back and the north wind blowing musical notes down the legs. It was beautiful, and I liked that it faced the dense woods between AJ's house and Oma's; that dark nothingness had never made me nervous, but I didn't like to turn my back on it. I scooped damp leaves from the chair and sat.

We called them thrones because, instead of canvas camp seats or whatever normal people had for outdoor furnishings, the fire pit was surrounded by these ornate stump chairs my Oma had made. Eighteen of them. The original six she made just after her youngest child left home: one for each of her four kids, one for my grandfather, and the one she'd carved for herself. Then later, one for each of their spouses except Uncle AJ's wife, Carmen (a source of great contention), and one for each of my nine cousins. One for every adult family member except for me, the youngest.

The grandchildren's chairs were added as a gift for each one's twentieth birthday, because Oma said kids weren't really people until then, and she couldn't carve a chair for you without knowing who you were. Her arthritis forced her to give up carving when I was sixteen. I never complained, since it felt petty to complain about a chair when she was losing the thing she'd spent her whole life on. But, still. Every time we assembled at the fire pit, which was most holidays and most summer weekends, I sat on a plain guest stump in the chilly outer tier alongside Aunt Carmen and tried to feel like I belonged.

I wasn't resentful; I just would have liked to know what she saw in me, like Jeremy's lion, or AJ's sea turtles, or my mother's planets. On the best of days, I walked around feeling like a puzzle piece in the wrong box, the one everyone looks at once in a while, then tosses back in hopes that it will somehow sort itself.

The dry wood crackled and sparked, burning fast despite damp air. Jeremy sat with his legs over one arm of his throne, a languorous royal leaving the work to the rabble, so I stood again to feed the fire. There was a thick shard in the kindling pile that I snagged and took to my seat, fishing in my pocket for my whittling knife. Something for my hands to do; I did the same when the musicians played.

We'd both done this a hundred times, though it had been years since he'd been in town for a family fire. Not that this was a family fire, with everyone else down in the house focused on food instead of music. Cheese crackers, stale beer, and the prodigal Jeremy amounted to a new combination.

The age difference was such that we'd never hung out alone before. He was the oldest son of the oldest sibling, and I was the second youngest's only child. It was a little awkward at first, both of us sticking to talk of AJ's absence and random family gossip, safe topics. Eventually we came around to me and my upcoming plans: another attempt at community college and then on to state university, better late than never.

"Aren't you too old to be a weather girl? Do you have what it takes?"

For a second, I hated him for the implication that I didn't have his drive, even though I knew it. He had jumped a bus to New York City the day before his senior-year English final, walked into some modeling agency, and gotten signed on the spot. Who tries that and actually succeeds? Only Jeremy. He was shooting an ad for designer jeans the day his classmates got their diplomas, and he never bothered to take his exams or the GRE or anything, even though he'd been a solid B student.

When he went from modeling to hosting *Haunt Sweet Home,* everyone just said, of course, that's Jeremy, whatever he wants to do will turn out perfectly for him. That's generally how it worked for everyone in my family, but he'd taken it further than most; he even had his own memes. The show itself was ridiculous: two people bought a house, and Jeremy hung out with them as they renovated it by day and slept in it by night, the latter always plagued by some kind of supposed haunting. Real? Fake? He always smiled and shrugged when you asked him.

His escape to the semi-big time made him a legend in our town. By the time I got to high school, seven years after he left, kids still saw my last name and asked if we were related; teachers too. His picture hung in our Hall of Fame, and he was listed on the school's Wikipedia page as the most famous alum, even though he'd never graduated. All of which swirled together in a complicated mix of annoyance and admiration in me.

Annoyance mostly. He wouldn't let up now that he thought he had my number, changing the timbre of his voice to match mine. "This is Mara Billings, reminding you to watch out for poodles, 'cause it's going to be raining cats and dogs today."

"I don't want to be a weather girl. Stop laughing at me." I punched him in the arm, which didn't do much of anything through his layers of expensive-looking wool. "Meteorology's not only for weather reports; I'm going to study climate science. Anyway, how many times have you made the 'this house has good bones' joke now? Or 'this house will put the boo in bougie'? You host a kitschy basic-cable show. People only watch you if they're stuck in the hospital and can't reach the remote to change the channel."

He closed his lips over his perfect teeth, trying to look serious; his dimples betrayed him. "Look, my kitschy basic-cable show needs a new production assistant. You can make, like, two hundred dollars a day running errands and restocking the craft table."

"You want me to bail on my degree to be your go-fer? You're going to lose some points with the parents." I extricated the last beer and tossed the cardboard case into the fire. I didn't want to sound too interested until I was sure he wasn't setting me up. If I said yes, wasn't I proving how easily I abandoned my plans?

"Not skipping out altogether; call it a gap year. It's not like you haven't bailed before. Isn't this your third time in community college?" He didn't wait for me to answer; it was my fourth. The last ten years had basically been a gap year. "And not a go-fer. PA is a cool job—a little of everything. Bottom rung of the production ladder, but you get to see how the magic happens, and you get to travel, and lodging is covered, so you don't have to pay rent on some shitty apartment. Take another break from school, work on our set, and maybe you can put away enough money that you won't have to go into fifty years of debt to be the next Al Roker or whatever. Do something different."

His "do something different" reminded me how long he hadn't been around. He'd missed years of aunts and uncles telling me to stop trying so many things and commit, and older cousins telling me to do what they had done, like I'd want to get compared to them forever. If I said yes, I'd be riding his coattails, but at least I'd be doing it somewhere else. I opened my mouth to ask for more details.

Brakes squealed in the driveway, announcing AJ's arrival even before his "What are you all doing here?" Which was followed by a slamming door, and then a lot of shouting, and then another slamming door, and a different car—no squeal—peeling out.

"Should we go see what's happening? I smell drama." Jeremy stood to put out the fire. I watched him, thinking about his offer.

There was indeed drama; we should have stayed outside with our crackers and beer. Uncle AJ had been hiking. He'd forgotten he told everyone at the Fourth of July cookout that he wanted to host Thanksgiving, forgotten he'd said he planned on getting a turkey-hunting license for the fall season, and that he'd take care of the bird. It was in line with the kind of things those siblings said, even if he'd never hunted turkey before; if they said they were doing something, they usually made it happen.

Everyone else remembered he'd said it, but somehow through all of the side-dish arrangements, through all the divorce messiness, nobody ever checked to see if he'd followed through. The departing car we'd heard was Aunt Bea, who ran all the stop signs down the hill into town to try to get to the supermarket before it closed for the holiday. She made it, barely, but there were no turkeys left, of course, and not even any whole chickens, so she ended up with a bunch of assorted chicken parts.

After which, all the parent-generation siblings and spouses had opinions on how to cook drumsticks and giblets to make them festive, made more difficult by the fact that AJ's oven had apparently given up the ghost, so they were trying to cook the meal using only a camping burner and a toaster oven. All three of his siblings lived within twenty miles, and Oma's place was practically next door, but nobody offered to move the holiday to another house; there was some unspoken consensus that we were toughing it out. They were all trying to be nice to AJ since he'd had a rough year, and exasperation permeated the air alongside the scent of whatever he'd cooked last in the toaster oven, congealed and burning on the bottom.

All that chaos, and when we finally bellied up to the buffet, shoveling food onto doubled-up paper plates, it was AJ who asked me in front of everyone if I was getting my act together to try college again, like his life was on track. Maybe he needed to highlight how one person in the family might be doing worse than him.

"I've got plans," I said, and headed for the kitchen. I meant to just grab a drink and clear my head for a sec, but someone in the living room said, "I've got plans to have some plans someday," and somebody else laughed, and not one relative defended me, not even my parents.

There were five pumpkin pies and four pecan on the kitchen table, way more than we needed, so I stacked my plate on top of one of the pumpkin ones, and walked out with dinner and dessert. I ate in my car in the dark, dinner and half a pie; nobody came looking for me.

I waited a week before emailing Jeremy to say hey, it was fun hanging out, and by the way, I thought about it and I've decided I'm interested in the job you mentioned. He responded saying sorry, it had already been filled. I kicked myself for not jumping on it right away; my usual self-sabotage.

Spring semester began. The other older students were all focused and determined, but every time I stepped into a classroom I felt like my teenage self, struggling again to stay awake through classes that didn't keep my attention; I stopped going after March break. BrewHaHa was happy to have me for more shifts. I wrote to Jeremy again in May, but this time it took him a month to respond. I think he was ignoring me because he hadn't wanted to say no again; now somebody had been fired right as they were about to start filming their new season in Massachusetts, and I had another chance.

I spent the drive to western Massachusetts listening to a podcast about *Haunt Sweet Home*. One host was a skeptic and one was a believer, and they brought on people with all kinds of theories about the show: it was staged; it was real; Jeremy killed people to make sure the houses were haunted; Jeremy was a ghost himself and responsible for all the hauntings. I made a mental note to tease him about that one.

I had binged a bunch of *HSH* episodes while I packed and it looked pretty hokey to me, but I was fascinated by the way the new homeowners always looked genuinely scared at the climax. ("Most episodes end with the new residents and their ghosts making peace," said the podcast guest who posited the Jeremy-as-ghost theory, "which is easy enough when your ghost is only being paid to haunt you for a week. It all makes perfect sense when you think about it.")

The navigation app had said the drive would take three hours, but the address I'd been given didn't distinguish North Mill Road from South Mill Road. I'd gone four winding miles in the wrong direction before a teenager at a farmstand told me to turn around. Luckily, I'd budgeted an extra hour for travel.

The house, when I finally found it, had the look I recognized from the show: a little grand, a little shabby, with "good bones," as Jeremy always joked. Not that I needed the haunted-house vibe to recognize the place, since there was a tent on the lawn, and the long driveway was crammed with two trailers and a dozen or so vans and cars. I parked behind a tan pickup with a Georgia vanity plate reading "L1GHTZ."

The L1GHTZ plate reminded me I was a total beginner among actual professionals. If I were starting school again, I'd be in a classroom with at least a few other students in the same boat, but here I was the only new person walking into a shoot full of reuniting colleagues. Colleagues who might think I'd only gotten the job because of my cousin; I hadn't really considered that. I'd been surfing the adrenaline of change up until the moment I realized it was a bigger wave than I'd experienced before; nothing to do but try not to drown.

One of the trailers had Jeremy's name on it, and the other said "Office" on the door, so I went there first to take care of my employment paperwork. I waited for the HR lady to tip her glasses and say something like "Jeremy told us all about you," but she didn't. She said, "It's nice to meet you—not that we'll be seeing much of each other, with you on graveyard shift." Which is how I found out I'd been hired as the production assistant for the night crew, not the day. Jeremy had neglected to mention that detail, or hadn't known which PA had been canned.

She went on to tell me a whole lot of stuff that Jeremy hadn't explained. That I'd be using my own car for errands. That everyone was union except for me. That I'd share my motel rooms with the day PA, but we would be on opposite shifts and wouldn't see each other. Those surprises were followed by a stack of tax forms and liability waivers, and then she directed me outside.

I stopped to knock on Jeremy's trailer on the way to the tent; nobody answered.

"Don't bother," called a burly white guy from across the lawn. He was piloting a dolly loaded with black cases. "If you need to reach him, ask one of the producers to text him."

I only had his email. We followed each other on social media too, so I could always direct message him on his Instagram or something. Or ask my mom to ask my aunt for his phone number, which involved way too many family members for my taste.

You know how sometimes you walk into a room and it's obvious everybody knows each other but you, and everyone looks your way at once? That was what I was expecting when I entered the lawn tent, but instead everyone ignored me except for a cluster at the far end, sitting around a table littered with coffee cups and hand-annotated printouts.

One of them, a Black woman with a welcoming smile, waved me over.

"You must be our new PA," she said when I approached. Her hair was pixie-short and she'd chopped the sleeves off her production T-shirt. Mid-twenties, probably, definitely younger than me, but with the confidence of someone who knew she was in the right job.

"Mara," I said.

"Nice to meet you. Lauren Andiamo, camera assistant. Welcome to the night crew."

She introduced the other people at the table: Lauren Tran, producer; Felix Johnson, director of photography; Buzz Eels, audio. None of them seemed as friendly as her; they all nodded and returned to their conversation.

She lowered her voice. "Don't worry about the two Laurens thing. Lauren Tran is Ms. Tran to all of us except Felix, and you can call me Andi. Fair warning, you'll probably be 'hey, you' to everyone. I'll try to call you by your name so you don't forget it."

I couldn't tell if I should laugh or not so I nodded, absorbing information. "So, all those other people work days?" That would explain why they didn't bother to look up; they weren't waiting on anybody new.

"Yeah." She started pointing around the room. "That's Joe Walsh, the day DP; everyone calls him Eagle for some reason. Kalima Musgrove, day producer. Then another Joe, Chris, Nadia, Joanna, Lori, Josie—camera, sound, drone pilot, safety, camera—incidentally, if you say 'Laur' or 'Joe,' chances are half the people in here will look up. So yeah, day crew is way bigger, even though a five-person night crew is pretty substantial for a show of our budget. A lot of shows don't have one at all, but on *HSH* we can't just set the cast up with diary cams and walk away."

I was hoping she was about to explain further, but we were interrupted by Ms. Tran. "You're my new PA?" She was shorter than me but somehow made me feel small when she turned her gaze my way. She looked me over, clearly a little surprised, though I wasn't sure why. I looked scruffy next to her, maybe, but so did pretty much everyone else, even though she was wearing the same T-shirt and jeans as the rest of the room, just in better fabrics and a more flattering cut.

"Yes, ma'am." I felt weird about the "ma'am" the second I said it. She was probably a little older than me, but not much.

"Welcome," she said. "It's not an easy job. The hours are long, we'll forget to thank you, and you'll know it when you fuck up. Be proactive. Don't talk to day about what we do at night; they're just a glorified construction crew and they wouldn't understand. Do everything I say, and also the things I haven't thought to tell you to do yet, but not the things I wouldn't tell you to do."

"Yes, ma'am." I hoped her last instruction would untangle itself in time.

When she walked away, Andi said, "She's direct, but she's not an abusive boss, I promise. And she's really, really good at her job. Everyone on night is. You'll see. We're like Seal Team Six, doing all the dirty work. Do you have any questions?"

I debated playing it cool, trying to figure things out from context, but that suddenly seemed like a recipe for disaster. Instead, I whispered, "What am I supposed to do? I have literally no idea. This is my first job that isn't at a coffee shop or a hardware store."

Her laugh wasn't directed at me, but more like I'd told a joke. "Honestly, if you can handle customer-facing stuff, you can handle this. Just assume when any of us says 'can someone get the *blah blah blah*,' the 'someone' is you."

We joined the conversation at the night crew table, or anyway she did, and I listened as they broke down how they thought the week's shooting would go. I looked around for Jeremy, but didn't see him anywhere.

When I asked Andi, she shrugged. "The Talent? He shows up when we need him on camera. He's probably not even in town yet."

"Does he do much with the night crew?"

"Like, one night per episode—so one night per week. We'll bring him in if there's something exciting happening, and otherwise manufacture something exciting."

Nobody had asked about my connection with Jeremy yet. Either he hadn't told them, or they didn't care; from Andi's attitude, it might be better if people didn't know. I was on my own for the first time ever. It was glorious.

2

Stonemill Farm hadn't been a working farm for ages. That was the first thing the producers told us at the 3 P.M. all-hands meeting. The original land had long ago been parceled off, leaving only the hundred-and-forty-year-old farmhouse and an overgrown lawn leading to a four-acre tangle of trees.

". . . But that's not all," whispered Andi to me as if we were already friends. "There's always a 'but that's not all.'"

"But that's not all," said the day producer. Andi grinned, and Kalima continued. "Nikita from the advance team poked their head around the area looking for any remnant of the mill the farm is named after."

"Ooh. We haven't had a haunted mill since season two," someone said.

"We've never done a mill. You're thinking of Fall's Bridge."

"No, not the bridge. He's thinking of the granary."

The producer forged on, ignoring the side conversation. "The overgrowth turns out to hide an apple orchard. We brought in an arborist who says it was planted in the twenties. She was amazed that it existed at all, even in its overgrown state, because behind a row of McIntosh and what she called 'old-school Red Delicious, not the tasteless kind from your school lunch,' most of the trees are Gravensteins."

Apparently New England's Gravenstein orchards were all killed over a bad winter in 1933–34, so now it was mostly thought of as a West Coast apple. Between the arborist's excitement and "the look of the trees," it had given the producers ideas. I was still trying to figure out how much of the show was scripted or contrived, though it was becoming clear that if a property didn't have a built-in ghost story already, it would have one soon enough.

After the producers spoke, we were all invited down to the orchard to look around. I couldn't tell if "all" included me, but Andi beckoned. The other members of the night crew stood at the edge of the larger group, and I stood at the edge of the night crew, like the time Oma took me to New York and we followed a paying group's tour guide around the Met, staying within earshot, never calling attention to ourselves.

The trees were taller than any apple trees I'd ever seen, and I'd seen a fair number in our part of Pennsylvania. Not giant for trees, but giant for apple, maybe twenty feet tall and almost as wide. The trunks were gnarled, some split into two or three parts by their own weight. Even though it was mid-July, the branches were heavy with apples; apparently Gravensteins were a summer crop. The ground was littered with bruised and rotting fruit, and hummed with happy bees. The sound guy took one look at the bees, shuddered, and turned back to the tent.

"Didn't you say his name was Buzz?" I asked Andi.

"It's triple ironic," she responded. "He's terrified of bees, and he barely ever talks, and he doesn't care at all about gossip. I can't even remember what his real name is, and he won't tell how he got the nickname, so don't ask. He's Buzz in the credits. Don't sing 'What's the Buzz?' at him, either. He's not a fan of Andrew Lloyd Webber."

I didn't know who Andrew Lloyd Webber was, so I filed that information away without too much concern. The arborist started talking about how, if it were her orchard, she'd bring the canopy down, and how she'd do it so fewer apples got bruised by their long fall, and fewer trunks split. She had a camera and mic on her as she walked, but Andi whispered, "They won't keep any of this. They'll keep the original interview where she said the orchard shouldn't exist and the rest will end up on the cutting room floor."

After the stroll, we moved as a group toward the house. My immediate impression was sunny and yellow, inside and out. A real farmhouse, someone said; functional, not fancy. We stepped into a bright living room, a dining area just beyond it with bay windows and doorways framed in dark wood, floors a lighter wood.

"Sometimes we have to suffer houses that have already been completely modernized inside," Andi whispered. "I'm glad this one got to keep some of its charm. Look at the hardwood."

The floors and beams did add a battered charm, up until we got to the kitchen. The appliances looked old like Oma's, but dirty, with food crusted on the burners and counters. Worse still, someone had carpeted the floor with something cheap and industrial, an angry mauve worn gray by spills and boot tracks.

"Carpet will go first, right?" I asked. "I feel like, in a lot of the episodes I've seen, you start by pulling up carpets if you think they're covering good floors."

Andi shrugged. "Yeah, we sometimes nudge the owners in that direction. It's easy and it changes the whole look of a room."

Someone opened a door that looked like it led to a closet or basement, and said, "Huh! Full bath off the kitchen."

Another person pointed at where the bathroom wall met the ceiling. "No crown molding along there. The bathtub used to be in the kitchen, before it got sealed off."

"It's the only full. There's just a toilet and sink upstairs."

Peering over shoulders, I observed a narrow bathroom with toilet, sink, and a dirt-ringed claw-foot tub with a shower attachment. A mildewed vinyl shower curtain bunched at one end of a track. The carpeting in here was in even worse shape than the kitchen's, moldering at the edges with years of sloshed water.

I wondered if they'd continued the hideous carpeting upstairs, but the floors up there were the same beautiful old wood as in the living room. The bedrooms smelled like patchouli, pot, and cat litter, and someone had left a tie-dyed tapestry tacked to one bedroom wall.

"I heard the last renters sold soap and candles at farmers' markets," somebody said.

"Have we ever done a hippie ghost? One that's angry because people aren't composting or something?"

"Put your groceries in rebooooooosable bags . . ."

Someone else laughed and put on a voice that sounded more like a vampire than a ghost. "Ve vant to separate your recycling . . ."

I turned to Andi. "What do we do when it's not creepy? Or when a house is fully modernized?"

"We film around it. It's all about angles and filters. In winter we can go a long way with a knocking radiator or flapping shutters." She pointed at the window, where both a paint-flaked radiator and a shutter rested in their passive state.

"Ugh," said a guy behind her. "We've done flapping shutters and creaky floors a thousand times. Please, run with something different. I beg you."

"It's not up to me," Andi said. "But I think this one will be different. We've never had a haunted orchard."

After the tour, everyone scattered as if they'd been given assignments I hadn't heard. I followed Andi toward the driveway, where she stopped at a newish Prius.

"What do we do now?" I asked. I was trying not to latch onto her too desperately, but she seemed like the safest person to ask questions.

"Day sets up for tomorrow morning, when the owners arrive and filming starts. Night doesn't actually have anything else to do before tomorrow evening, so we can check into the motel and relax. Normally we'll eat dinner together when we wake up—catch up on what happened during the day and what we'll be doing that night—but tonight we're on our own."

She got in her car, ending the conversation. I walked down the long driveway to the hatchback I'd saved up to buy from my cousin Ollie after high school. Ancient then, more ancient now. In the car, I riffled through paperwork until I found the name of the motel. I could've followed Andi, I supposed, but she hadn't offered. On our own.

It wasn't far, anyway. A few stop signs, a merge onto an empty highway, four exits, and then the sign for the Mountainview Motel sticking up tall enough to see from the highway's elevation.

Jeremy had said I'd get to travel, but apparently he meant we'd spend the whole season commuting between various houses in western Massachusetts and our base at a cheap-ass motel the production company had rented out. The Mountainview Motel's name was a lie; it had views of highways, parking lots, a school, and a gas station. At least there was water in the pool.

I didn't own much, so unpacking wasn't difficult. I'd borrowed an old suitcase from my parents and filled it with ancient black jeans and black T-shirts left over from building theatre sets in high school; I'd figured correctly the wardrobe for this job would be the same. Then a swimsuit, enough underwear to keep me from having to wash laundry too often, and my one nice black dress in case of emergency, which I hung in the closet. Camping gear stayed in the car.

The production office had said I'd have a roommate, so I unpacked into the side of the double dresser that was closer to the door. I lined my toiletries up neatly on one corner of the sink, then changed into my swimsuit.

The motel wrapped around the pool on three sides, but the whole place looked deserted. I relaxed into my steady backstroke, eyes on the cloudless sky, enjoying the solitude after the stress of meeting new people. Twenty laps in, I touched flesh instead of wall when I started my flip, and came sputtering up for air. Andi sat with her legs dangling into the water, wearing board shorts and a sports bra. "You're a good swimmer."

"I love swimming. My cousins were all on the swim team, but I've always considered it a solitary thing. Me and a lake, or me in the high school pool after the teams go home." More information than she'd asked for.

She stood. "I can leave you to it."

"No! There's plenty of room for both of us. I just meant it's nice that there aren't a dozen people in here."

"I get it. I like to run on my own." She slipped into the water, and relief washed over me that I hadn't offended the only person who'd given me the time of day.

After we'd both swam separately for a while, she settled on a floral-cushioned lounge chair. I did a few more laps, then rested with my arms in the gutter. "Can I ask a stupid question?"

"No question too stupid. Well, possibly, but I'll answer anyway, and laugh on the inside."

She was honest, at least. "I'd think if you were going to put your new house on a show called *Haunt Sweet Home*, a show you'd applied to be on, a show you'd presumably watched a time or two given that we're filming the seventh season, you'd go in too skeptical to be scared. How do people not anticipate what's coming? They always look genuinely terrified."

"Did you watch *Mad Men*?"

I shook my head.

"There's this scene where somebody's foot gets run over by a lawnmower at a party. The other actors were told the crew would be throwing fake blood at them on the count of three, but the director quietly arranged for the blood to be thrown on 'two' instead of 'three.' They got this amazing reaction shot because the surprise was real. No anticipation.

"It's like that. They don't know *how* they'll be scared, so it still catches them by surprise. The editing on the finished product makes it feel inevitable and obvious, like if you talk a lot about the boarder who threw himself out the attic window, then of course it's going to be a creaky attic episode. But the owners don't know the research we've done, not until Jeremy says, 'I looked into your house's history, and I've discovered . . . ,' and they don't know which things talked about during the day will be reinforced by their friendly neighborhood night crew. They get scared because there are no special-effects people listed in our credits, so it must be real. And they get scared because there's a difference between watching creepy stuff on television and having it happen to you."

She grinned. "You have legit just stumbled into the coolest job in the world. Day does the usual formulaic pre-scripted reality TV stuff, like filming the owners pretending to walk into their new house for the first time, and getting fake candid shots of them relaxing after a busy day of renovation, and doing all the actual renovations, and interviewing them about what they'd just said in all the previous footage. Then *we* get to convince them their new purchase is genuinely haunted. You're going to love it. I hope you love it. I love it."

I returned her smile. "How could I not after a pitch like that?"

The sun dried us off. After my shower, I DMed Jeremy to ask which room he was in and if he wanted to grab dinner, then checked his socials. His most recent Instagram post was a selfie at lunch that day in Brooklyn; Andi had been right when she said he wasn't in town yet. I thought about knocking on her door to ask if she wanted to scrounge some food, but I already felt like I'd bothered her too much. Anyway, I'd have to skimp until our first payday, which was easier when food wasn't social.

Instead, I dashed across the empty road and grassy median to the gas station. Inside the tiny convenience store, a sign over a chest fridge proclaimed SANDWICHES MADE FRESH DAILY, but they looked suspiciously fuzzy. I bought a Coke and a frozen burrito and heated the latter in a nest of tissues in the motel room microwave. The microwave made the overhead lights dim, and it took four times the recommended time listed on the wrapper.

While I ate my soggy burrito, I started listing things to buy: paper towels, protein bars, ramen, bread, peanut butter. Maybe it would be better to find a store right then, before we got busy, but a day of new experiences had drained me.

I was in bed watching reruns of our show for research when a key rattled the lock and the door opened, only to be caught by the security chain. "Hey!"

"I'm sorry! I wasn't thinking!" I jumped to unlock it, then stood awkwardly face-to-face with a tiny woman who looked like she was trying to erase me from existence with her eyes.

"Who the fuck are you? Ugh. Don't tell me they gave me a roommate again. You look really old for a PA."

I didn't say anything. It hadn't occurred to me that my entry-level job was probably usually filled by people ten years younger than me. Maybe that was why Ms. Tran had looked at me strangely too.

My roommate pushed past me and tossed two duffels on the second bed. "For the future, pretend the door chain doesn't exist. It isn't our friend."

"Do you need help? I can carry stuff."

"Nah. Just don't lock me out again." She ducked out and returned a second later with another bag, a ukulele case, a hot plate, and a couple of Chinese food boxes in a plastic bag, which she stuffed into the mini-fridge.

"At least you look like you know how to share space." She started to unpack into the drawers and closet. "The last one left stuff all over the sink, and she dressed herself out of her luggage through the whole shoot. It made me anxious, like I was living with a spy, always prepared to take off at a moment's notice."

"Is that what she did? Took off?"

"No, actually. She got canned when a flood warning went off on her phone in the middle of a scene. We're not supposed to have our phones with us when we're shooting, let alone have them turned on. Anyway, at least she didn't have any packing to do; she was right about having to leave quickly."

She had stopped shooting eye daggers at me, so I took the opportunity to introduce myself. "Was that right at the end of the season? I heard I was replacing somebody. I'm Mara, by the way."

"Cath Ruiz. And no, I didn't mean 'the last one' like 'the last night PA.' I actually meant 'the last night PA who shared a room with me.' When she got fired halfway through last season, someone else suggested a friend of his, a guy, so I got a room to myself for the last few weeks. I guess I was hoping he'd hung around." She spoke as if she was used to having to get everything she had to say out in one breath. "Oh, I should apologize in advance for tonight. I snore. If you don't have earplugs I think I have an extra pair. This is pretty much the only night you'll have to deal with it, unless you stick around on weekends. You're not sticking around on weekends, are you?"

"No," I said, then immediately regretted it. Here I was already agreeing to what somebody else needed from me instead of what I needed, just like at home.

"Live nearby?"

"A couple of hours. I was thinking of doing some camping." True enough, though I hadn't planned on every weekend.

"I'll bet there're great places to camp in this area. I've never been here before—it's pretty."

"Where did you film last season?" The most recently filmed episodes hadn't aired yet, and I couldn't remember what Jeremy had said.

"Georgia. Gorgeous houses, but the location scouts had a rough time finding old sites that weren't built on or maintained with slave labor, which wasn't a narrative we wanted to exploit for the show. We mostly did newer places and stayed away from the grounds. I don't think we'll film down there again anytime soon."

Cath finished unpacking her clothes. She pulled a game console from a padded bag and connected it to the television on the dresser, then made one more trip to her car for a green plastic tub, which she put on the other side of the TV.

She pointed at the tub. "Snacks. The last motel had mice so I invested in a little protection. Feel free to help yourself, and to keep your own food in there. Just put your name on anything you don't want me to touch and I'll do the same. Ditto for the fridge."

"Cool," I said. "I was going to find a store tomorrow. Let me know if there's anything you want me to grab for you."

"I loaded up before I got here. Don't bother with granola bars or fruit. You can steal those from the craft table. I'm the one who stocks the table, so just tell me what you want and it'll appear. That's most of what's in my snack tub, anyway."

I nodded. I'd never had a roommate before, but she seemed pretty agreeable once we got past her initial dismay. Up until the snoring started; it cut right through my borrowed earplugs. I spent an hour in the dark stressing over not getting enough sleep before I realized I didn't actually have to be on set until late afternoon. I watched movies on my phone until I couldn't keep my eyes open. Her alarm blared at 5 A.M. and woke me, but I dozed off again and when I woke for real she was gone and it was almost noon.

There turned out to be a Walmart two towns over, so I bought the stuff on my list, minus granola bars. My fuel light came on two miles from the motel, and I cursed myself for wasting gas on getting lost the day before. I put ten dollars in the tank, hoping I wouldn't get asked to drive around too much before payday.

After the errands I swam, then tried unsuccessfully to nap. The first night would be a long one, with my internal clock on its normal settings, but hopefully my body would make the switch soon enough.

We'd been told to meet at the motel restaurant at 6 P.M. I ate a peanut butter sandwich so I wouldn't have to pay for a full dinner—I could just say I wasn't hungry and order fries or soup or something. I opened the shade enough to see out and sat on my bed ready to go, one eye on the window. When Andi passed, I slipped out the door as if I'd just been on my way as well, what timing.

"Hey," I said from a few feet behind her.

She turned and waited for me to catch up. "Hey! You ready?"

"I think so. Didn't sleep much."

"It's hard to catch the rhythm at first, but you'll get there."

I nodded. "How come we're meeting here instead of at the house?"

"Mostly so we can talk about the owners without worrying they'll overhear. It's harder to communicate over there. Day has it a little easier, since they tend to follow a pattern for the week, but we usually need to confer and strategize ahead of time—you'll see.

"The other reason is so Ms. Tran can expense dinner for us. It's what we call a silent perk. It doesn't happen every night, but some. If Ms. Tran makes the invitation, she's paying; if anyone else does, assume you are."

I regretted having eaten the sandwich.

The restaurant was called Lulu's Family. An Indian teenager greeted us at the PLEASE WAIT TO BE SEATED sign. "Are you with the TV crew? The six o'clock reservation?"

On Andi's assent, she walked us through the large empty dining room to a smaller private one, also empty, with six plate settings and six menus. "This will be reserved for your group any time you need it, unless we have a birthday party or something. I'm Sathya. I'll be your server all summer. Can I get you anything to drink?"

I ordered a Coke and Andi ordered coffee. When Sathya returned with our drinks, she was followed by the others from the night crew.

"Early birds," said Ms. Tran, nodding with what seemed

like approval. She sat at the head of the table, and the men took the remaining seats.

"Diner food and Indian?" Felix fanned himself with the menu. "I'm in heaven."

"I love the idea of getting tandoori chicken and a milkshake," said Buzz. It was the first time I'd heard him speak.

"That's what lassis are for?"

"Lassis are great. So are coffee milkshakes. I have room for both in my heart."

I stayed quiet, listening to the easy banter of people who had worked together before. Nobody had given me so much as a look, which I was fine with. I studied the menu and tried to come up with choices in two different price ranges, since I wasn't sure how much I was allowed to spend. I'd had Indian food a few times in middle school at my friend Aarti's house and liked it, but I'd never known the names of anything her mom made.

The others ordered entrées from the Indian side of the menu, so I followed their lead, feeling pleased with myself until Sathya asked, "How much spice?" and turned to me first. I said "none," and then everyone else said "medium." I thought I saw Ms. Tran smirking at me, so I said, "It makes sense to me not to order anything too spicy before my first night of a job where I don't know how often I'm allowed to take bathroom breaks."

"Good logic," Andi said. "Nobody really wants to be around after Buzz eats spicy food. Don't let anyone pressure you."

Nobody else laughed, and I decided they were all okay. In truth, if it had been the other way around and everyone had said "medium" before it was my turn, I probably would have said it just to blend in. It wasn't until the next night that I noticed the options were printed as spicy, medium, and mild, and maybe they were just laughing because I'd said "none" instead of "mild."

While we waited for our food, Ms. Tran profiled the owners. "They're two tech bros from Boston—well, one is from Iowa and one is from New York, but they live in Boston. They were in a frat together at MIT, and made some money developing a farmers' market app. Not zillionaire money. It tells you how to find farmers' markets, or what they have in season or something, and it also helps farmers run their CSAs. Now they want to restore this house and orchard. Maybe as a business later; just for fun for now.

"Matthew Chen is the one from Iowa; he's the one who found the house. Hart Thatcher is Upper East Side. Old money, I think. He'd wanted another place they saw, but it cost more and had less acreage. He's a little hung up on the fact they are two grown-ass adult men platonically buying a three-hundred-thousand-dollar house together and they don't even get their own bathrooms. He wants to get started on expanding the half bath right away, but Matthew wants to start with that god-awful kitchen because, and I quote, 'grown-ass adult men have gotten by with a whole lot less. There are two toilets and we can take turns with the shower, but we need to be able to cook a meal without getting food poisoning from the counters.'"

"I like this guy," said Andi. "Very practical."

"Let's get to the important part already," said Buzz. "How are we using the orchard?"

The food arrived, and we paused to distribute it. Ms. Tran had ordered naan for the table, and I was eager to show I at least knew what to do with that. I said silent thanks to Aarti and her mother, wherever they were. When we'd eaten a bit, Felix spoke. "So, the orchard . . . I've got a few things planned. You're not afraid of the dark, are you, new PA?"

"Someone probably should have asked her that question before now," said Andi.

I didn't say that I hadn't even been told I was hired for night shift, since saying that would involve telling them how I'd gotten the job. "I grew up playing in the woods."

"So, let me tell you the plan," said Felix, without acknowledging that I'd spoken. It didn't seem like the plan would be any different if I'd said the opposite. Anyway, it was true. We often got sent out into the woods between AJ's and Oma's. Everyone else was so much older than me, and I was constantly getting left behind to figure my own way. I'd learned not to panic, because they all got annoyed if they had to come find me.

After dinner, Felix shifted a storage tub from his room to my backseat, and then I took him to Walmart, since apparently he was the only one among us who didn't drive. I was conscious of my check-engine light, though at least I'd gotten enough gas to turn off the low-fuel alert.

He was friendlier one-on-one; it turned out he knew all kinds of awesome practical effects, which he enthused about on our drive. We bought a cooler and ice and stood in the store parking lot while he cut holes in either end of the cooler. His tub in my backseat held a battery-operated fog machine, and he demonstrated how to pump some liquid he called "fog juice" over ice in the cooler so the fog would stay low and billow out between the trees toward the house instead of dissipating upward. I'd seen mysterious mists on the show before; now I knew how that particular magic happened. So much for ghosts.

"Park here," Felix said, just before we reached the driveway. "If we carry everything through the woods from this side, we won't risk anyone at the house seeing us."

Dusk had fallen during his fog demonstration, and it was fully dark now. I turned my hazards on since the road where we'd pulled over had no shoulder, then switched them off again at his frown. Maybe if my car got hit on the job, the production would pay for me to buy a vehicle manufactured in this century. Or maybe I should have read all those waivers more closely.

I hoisted the ice-filled cooler, heavy and awkward. I didn't want to complain about anything on my first day, so I just gritted my teeth, thinking of how buff I'd be after a couple of months of this.

If I wasn't allowed hazard lights on the car, Felix definitely wouldn't approve of a flashlight; I didn't have a free hand to hold one in any case. We had to cross a drainage ditch and a stand of pines to get to the orchard. The ditch was dry, at least, and the moon filtering through the trees was still bright enough to let me mostly see where I was going, except for what was directly ahead, blocked by the cooler. I tripped as we approached the orchard.

"You okay?"

"Yeah, just some rubble."

Felix looked down. "What's left of a stone wall. Odd that it's out here, not near the apple trees; I wonder what it marked."

He toed some underbrush out of the way, following the border. I watched as his posture changed; he was clearly excited about something.

"What?" I asked.

"Look for more stones—over here, this side. You can put down the cooler."

I did as I was told. This patch was filled with vines and weedy trees—holly, I discovered when it raked my arms, and mulberry—but beneath those were more stones. Gravestones: we'd found a cemetery. A cemetery old enough to have sunken and grown over and eroded; erased.

"Do you see any names?" he asked.

"No," I said. "I think they're all too worn to read even if it wasn't dark out."

It took some searching, but we eventually found a partial stone still standing, like a single snaggletooth in a mouth full of broken ones. The shard read HAN and below that 18, but it was impossible to tell whether the "18" was part of a birthdate or death date, a year or century.

"Could be a first or last name," I said. "Or a pet."

He ignored the pet part. "This is great! We'll finish setting up for tonight like I planned, and then Lauren can decide whether to tell the day crew to send the owners to 'discover' this tomorrow, or to lure them out here tomorrow night. Either way, this is story gold."

Felix left the cemetery reluctantly, glancing back one more time. The twisted, overgrown apple branches caught my hair and scratched my face as I followed him into the orchard proper.

We stopped four rows in and eight trees from the edge. I didn't see any reason he'd chosen that particular place, but

Felix pointed across the lawn. "You can see the house from here, but to them this will just be a tangle. Will you be able to find your way here again alone? No flashlight? We can get your car off the road, but you still have to come in from the side, not the lawn, so nobody sees you."

I pictured the ditch, the cemetery, the low branches, and nodded; easy enough to count rows and locate the equipment again now that I'd done it once. We found our way back to the car and I drove us up to where the others were parked, as if we hadn't stopped along the way. Since we were so late, I didn't get to meet the owners. Felix said it was just as well; if I was beneath their notice, they also wouldn't notice my absences.

For the next couple of hours I was kept busy with "hey, you" stuff, pretty straightforward. They filmed the owners, Matt and Hart, arguing over who got the master bedroom, with its bay windows and massive built-in armoire. Ms. Tran managed to convince them both to sleep in there and decide who it belonged to later. I don't think they recognized they were being manipulated, but I could see why she did it: easier to film them in one room; easier to infect each other with fear's contagion in one room. She set up an interview spot with the armoire as backdrop, giving them a view across the lawn and down to the orchard through the bay window. They inflated two mattresses in the room's center.

A little after midnight, Felix nodded, cueing me to slip out of the house. I walked to the tent as if I'd been told to get something, then ducked under the back flap so it would shield me from view if anyone looked out; the same angles that had been set to force their view toward the orchard would expose me if I wasn't careful. I didn't want to mess things up my first night.

I didn't have to go far into the trees to conjure the feeling that I was alone; I heard crickets, and an owl somewhere far off, but no voices, no cars, no machines at all. The absence of human sounds struck me as a lovely thing after two long days of learning new names and faces and rules.

The dark orchard didn't scare me; it reminded me of home. Different trees, different textures underfoot, but the same enveloping darkness. The same shift to reliance on a different set of senses.

I was suddenly glad for all the time I'd spent in the woods behind Oma's house, searching for deadfall to drag back to her workshop, trying to find my way home after the others forgot I was following them. Was everyone who took this job as comfortable out here? Maybe other seasons didn't start outdoors, and simply required no fear of attics or basements. Maybe this was why the position had come open twice since Jeremy had first asked me.

I counted rows and found the equipment we'd left a few hours earlier. The fog machine had faded into the darkness, but the cooler's white lid made it easy to spot; we should probably have covered it in leaves. I sat on it, with my back against a tree, and waited for the appointed fog time.

When I stood again, I bashed my shoulder on a branch and an apple fell at my feet. Nobody had said anything about not eating them, and they were all just going to waste. I polished it on my shirt and bit in.

I'd never tasted a Gravenstein before. It was perfectly ripe, honey sweet with a hint of tartness. A dribble of juice trickled down my chin, and I wiped it with my arm. I was standing in an orchard in the middle of the night eating apples off the tree and getting ready to make my first attempt at scaring people for a living; one of the better situations I'd found myself in lately.

At 12:43 I followed Felix's directions and started the fog, which did what it was supposed to, hugging the ground as it crept between the trees and out toward the house. After, I skirted the lawn coming around to the driveway and hung out in my car for another hour so they wouldn't associate my disappearance and appearance with the timing of the fog. I desperately wanted to close my eyes, but I didn't want to risk sleeping longer than I should and losing the job on the first night.

Before I finally headed back to the production tent, I grabbed a case of bottled water from the van as Felix had suggested, so it would look like I'd left with a purpose, if the owners noticed me. Buzz dozed with his head on a table, his hand still clutching his insulated coffee mug. Andi and Felix were playing cards, and Ms. Tran was reading something on her phone—she was the only one allowed to have one on set, because the rule against them was hers to break.

Andi smiled when I entered, and whispered to me that it had looked awesome. The moon was almost full, so the fog had really stood out against the dark orchard. I asked if the owners were asleep, and she pointed at the bedroom, where a flashlight threw flickering arcs across the room.

We interrupted them again half an hour later for another interview and then again at four. The guys were punchy and irritable but not particularly unsettled. We let them fall asleep just before dawn, at which point I returned for the cooler and fog machine so they wouldn't find evidence if they went exploring during the day. I think I also would have been punchy and irritable if I'd had to talk to anyone at that point, and my head felt disconnected from my body as I trudged through the orchard. My eyes closed a couple of times, involuntarily, but each time, a branch whacked me in the face and reminded me I needed all senses on deck if I was going to walk around in the dark.

We went to Denny's for breakfast around six, a meal where literally nobody spoke other than to order food. Ms. Tran didn't say anything about paying, so I ordered an omelet and then cut it in two so it would last for another meal, even though I was famished. I ate all the toast and potatoes.

Back at the motel, there was a note on the table from Cath saying she hoped I'd had a good first night and that she'd accidentally exploded ramen in the microwave but she'd clean it in the evening, sorry about the smell.

I crashed until five, when I jumped in the pool and swam a few laps, then showered in time for our crew meeting at Lulu's. Since it was an official meal, I ordered another Indian dish and a milkshake.

Ms. Tran started the meeting saying my fog had done its job.

Andi threw a fry at me. "She's terrible at compliments. You did great. We got a really good panic shot from one of them. He thought he saw a man in the branches. Then the other one freaked out because yesterday's weather shouldn't have been conducive to fog."

I ate the thrown fry slowly, wondering if that was true. I only knew a little about fog, mostly in relation to environmental stuff, like how there's a town in Peru with no lakes or rivers or wells, so they installed these big fog-catcher screens that collect hundreds of gallons of water.

Felix interrupted my straying thoughts. "Why would we care what real weather does? It's supposed to be haunted fog."

"Yeah, that's what the first guy pointed out to his buddy," Andi agreed. "We didn't even need to intervene."

Ms. Tran smiled. "The day crew said it was all they could talk about in their rise-and-shine."

That sounded like a better compliment. I asked Andi later, and she said the rise-and-shine was the first interview of the morning, deliberately filmed in the first golden rays of sun, pre-coffee and pre-shower to maximize exhaustion.

"Did they get sent out to explore today?" I hadn't been late to the meeting, but I was still the last to the table, and everyone else already seemed more in the know than me. Maybe because I was the bottom rung, or maybe because my night kept me running around so much it was harder to keep the plot.

Ms. Tran waved her fork. She'd been picking raw mushrooms out of her salad, and one bit flew from the tines. "They did. Day made sure they found your little cemetery. They also sent Cath into town records since the advance research team had missed it, but she came up empty, so it probably was just for pets, or else it predated the orchard and house by enough time to have been forgotten. I'm sure there's some Hans who died in this town at some point though, even if he didn't have any connection with the house. We can lean into that."

"He could be a jilted lover," Felix said. "Haunting the orchard where he and his fiancée courted."

"Cliché."

We all looked at Buzz, who rarely spoke, and waited for him to say more. When he didn't, Ms. Tran nodded. "Yeah, I think we did that plot in season four. What about a boy who fell while picking apples?"

"The buyer said he saw a man though, not a boy?" I said it cautiously, as a question, since I wasn't entirely sure I was allowed to contradict the boss.

"Good point. A migrant worker who fell picking apples? A migrant might not make it into town records."

"Were there migrants then?"

"A hobo stealing apples? During the depression?"

"Is 'hobo' still an okay term to use?"

Felix shook his head. "These trees would only have been babies then. Too small to climb, let alone fall from, for a farm worker or a hobo or even a kid. And the stone looks older, anyway."

"He doesn't need to have climbed. Maybe he was a hobo they'd taken in, and everyone liked him, and something tragic happened, like he was allergic to bee stings, and after he died they realized nobody even knew his last name. Or a traveling salesman? Those dudes in the house would relate."

"Melancholy!" Felix was ecstatic. "Melancholy is so much more interesting than evil."

"I like melancholy better too," said Andi. "They have to live in the house after we're done shooting, so I'd always rather leave them feeling sorry for their ghost than scared of it."

"I'm okay with either and both, so long as it keeps people watching." Ms. Tran had the final word on the subject.

They tossed ideas around the table, and a few more fries.

I still didn't feel confident enough to say much, so I listened as they hashed out the details of poor Han's life, death, and afterlife: not a hobo, but a farm worker, in an older orchard planted long before the current one. Felix and Ms. Tran both seemed to have a general philosophy that the team did better work when they—we—had a common vision.

Eventually, the conversation came around to what they had planned for me. I'd start with another midnight fog, then wave a flashlight through the fog and the branches, at an angle to the house. The owners in the 1890s were the Day family, so Buzz would record himself saying "Miss Day? Miss Day?" in his radio baritone, and I'd broadcast him from the orchard. It was a Rorschach recording, since "Miss Day" could also be heard as "mistake?" which seemed like a good thing for a ghost to repeat. Buzz said it might also sound like "mist, eh?" but the others agreed only a Canadian would think that.

Darkness fell and I got to do my fog thing, then hauled the evidence to my car. Afterward, the flashlight bit, and a little later, Buzz's recording, which sounded suitably creepy calling out between the trees. That took us to about 2 A.M. Ms. Tran had ordered me to stay hidden in case the owners decided to explore. If they did, I'd break branches and play Buzz's recording a few more times, while keeping a healthy distance.

I sat under a tree for a while and listened for the front door, or voices, but nobody came. Waited long enough to feel like the only thing haunting the orchard was me. I wouldn't have minded closing my eyes, but falling asleep and letting the owners discover me there would be as instant a sacking as letting my phone ring. I couldn't even read; the moon was still bright, but those big old Graven-steins had too thick a canopy for its light to filter down to me. All I could do was wander between the trees, listening for the house and keeping an eye out in its general direction, which I did until I tripped and sent myself sprawling. Not a bad fall; I didn't hit my head, though I gave my right wrist a jolt and scraped my palms enough to bleed.

The tree I'd tripped over must have been struck by lightning at some point, the way it had split. One side was still standing, but at a steep angle. The roots had broken through the ground, like fingers from the grave—those were what had caught me. About a third of the trunk had cleaved away, held upright by the next tree over. Two dead branches looked like arms reaching toward me, and for a moment I took it for a person. Even after my eyes made sense of what I was looking at, there was something expressive about it. I knew how I was going to spend the rest of the long night.

3

My oma used to whittle spoons and birds from scraps of wood my cousins and I found for her.

"How do you know which parts to cut away?" I asked her once.

"I ask it what it wants to be. If I look at it long enough, I see the shapes inside. Do you see anything in this one?"

I examined what I'd brought her, a soft-curved splinter of pine. "A dove?"

She nodded, taking me seriously, then coaxed the bird from the wood. Not an exact replica, but the spirit of the thing. If I had said "a duck" or "a hummingbird," I imagine she'd have made that instead, but it was magic to me as a kid.

She'd offered to teach us all how to do it ourselves. My cousins passed on the offer, and my mother said I was too young for knives; by the time I was old enough, Oma's arthritis had gotten worse, and she couldn't hold her tools properly anymore. She still taught me a little, ducks and spoons, but it was more talking than hands-on instruction by then, and I've always learned better by doing than listen-and-learn. I practiced on my own sometimes.

I wasn't supposed to show my face for at least an hour,

and this deadwood definitely looked like it had a shape to reveal, if I could only draw it out. I reached into my backpack for my multi-tool.

This was a boredom-reliever that wouldn't get me in trouble as long as I kept my ears open. A project. A huge project, not really right for a beginner working at night on limited time. I didn't have the skill to pull off anything beyond basic—more ducks, more spoons. Like everything else in my life, I'd dabbled but never committed. Not like my grandmother.

Oma learned it from her own mother, who had carved reliefs, banisters, mantels, altars. Fine-art stuff, formal, designed to last centuries. Oma's brother, my great-uncle, became a luthier, and my grandmother carved everything from decorative birds and animals to full-sized stuff like our fire pit chairs, to her own less representative fine art. She had exhibits at the museums that understood her, alongside O. L. Samuels, Antonio Alberti, Fred Carter; so-called visionary artists.

She sold the commercial stuff from a little one-room store in her front yard until she couldn't sculpt anymore. AJ kept pushing her to learn 3-D rendering, which he said was the same as what she did, but she said plastic held no shapes to reveal. He also pushed her to sell online, which she wouldn't do, and to sell other people's work, which she wouldn't do, and to design custom work on other people's specifications, which she wouldn't do, even when it was clear the end of her own carving would mean the end of her store.

She told him she had no interest in computers. She opened her store three days a week from twelve to three for thirty-eight years, and carved new items while she waited for customers to buy the ones already on the shelves. People sought out her little shop because everything she made was one of a kind, even if some of it was kind of weird. She took special orders, but only from people who supplied their own wood and carried no preconceived notion about its ultimate form.

For her last four months in business, she sat behind the counter with her stand fan blowing and NPR keeping her company, and two pieces left on the shelf: an abstract twist and a one-legged duck, the last art she'd made before her arthritis got too bad to keep going. My dad finally paid one of his friends to go in and buy both. That was 2:15 P.M. on a Tuesday. She turned her OPEN sign to CLOSED, walked up the drive to the house, and never set foot in the shop again.

The main thing I took away was her insistence on allowing the wood to dictate the shape. She listened or looked or held it until a new form revealed itself, but she never started with any plan for what she wanted to create that day, even if she knew the duck festival was coming, or Christmas, or whatever. You couldn't ask her to make a portrait of your dog. Sometimes she'd stare at the wood for hours, or run her finger along the grain of it with her eyes closed, like she was reading it in Braille. When she finally cut, it could become anything. Ducks or strange swirls, or faces pushing through the wood like they were coming out of the water, or animals I didn't recognize. She said it wasn't hers to question what a piece wanted to be.

I stood in the darkness waiting for the shattered apple tree to speak to me. What did wood sound like when it spoke to my grandmother? A sound, or a feeling, or a clearing away of everything except the true shape?

My first thought was that the tree looked a little like the bow of a ship, a figurehead. The curve was right, but the idea soured, clashed. I was imposing my own ideas, and besides, the tree wasn't going anywhere; it didn't need someone to guard its passage.

I stared again, trying to conjure Oma's way of looking. "What are you?" I asked, and waited. I asked again, and this time, I heard an echo of my words twist around the trees and back to me in my own voice. *What are you? Are you? You?*

It felt accusatory at first, like I didn't have a right to be doing this, like my question had been turned around on me. My whole family was good with our hands, but I had no skill, no practice at this beyond my idle whittlings. This beautiful tree deserved someone better than me. If she were still carving, I'd have taken it straight to Oma, do not pass go. But she wasn't, and nobody else in the family worked with this kind of thing, and who was to say I couldn't be good at it if I tried.

Maybe I was tired, but just then something shifted in my sight, and I recognized the human shape in the wood. The branches I had initially pictured as creepy arms were unnecessary Halloween-store scares; the arms were meant to follow the lines of the body, rather than reaching. The shape held a tension, a taut wire from the head to where the torso burst from the stump. Not pleading, but beseeching. Searching. Transforming. It wasn't me, but there was some quality of me in the shape, anger at my own self-doubt, at my own inability to know myself. All right there in the wood, waiting, calling to me. *What are you? Are you? You?*

Whether I could draw it out was another question. Oma had an array of tools I'd never even learned the names of.

Maybe, maybe, some understanding of wood ran in my family, but Oma had always called bullshit on the idea of propensity. What we had, she said, was an agreement that wood held beauty, and an understanding of the multitude of ways to release beauty from wood. All of which took time; I had a multi-tool and a whittling knife, a little bit of practice, and the promise of, at best, a few hours a night for the next few nights.

I did what I could.

The wood was dry and cool to my touch; it had been an arid summer. The easy part came first: cutting away what definitely didn't belong. Severing the Halloween arms was a nerve-wracking gamble, since there was a chance I'd ruin the piece before I'd even begun, but I looked again, and it felt right. I persevered, separating what wasn't part of my sculpture from what was.

Hard going, even at this crude shaping stage; I tried to remember Oma's hierarchy of woods. White pine was easy. She had a rhyme she'd made up so we'd remember what to bring her and what not to bother with.

> Basswood, butternut, cedar, pine
> walnut, cherry, you'll do fine

Apple wasn't on her list. When I looked it up online the next morning, I discovered the woodworking community's consensus that apple was beautiful and worth the trouble, but not for beginners. Durable, beautiful, dense. Still; they didn't say impossible, just difficult. Maybe I could make something special. Said I, the beginner.

It turned out to be more time-intensive than I expected,

but I had time to kill. A little fog, a little flashlight, a little "just press play" on the spooky recording. On Wednesday the homeowners were encouraged to explore in the dark, and I spent an hour dodging the two men and our trailing film crew. Felix had planned for that to be the night they went proactive, so I'd only brought the recording, not the fog machine.

I didn't realize my mistake until they were stalking me through the trees: if the owners found my rough carving while wandering, it would be a divergence from the loose script we'd been following. I crept around them a couple of rows away, played the recording again, and managed to lead them toward the cemetery, which worked out well for everyone. The crew got a whole lot of bleep-worthy dialogue from both guys, and one of them gave a heartfelt promise to Han, whoever he was, to figure out what the ghost needed from them. If nothing better came the next night, this could be edited into a solid climax for the episode.

We wrapped at Stonemill Farm on Friday. In the pre-dawn hours, I crept into the orchard with an ax I'd borrowed from the day crew carpenter, and severed the last connections between the deadwood of my carving and the trunk's living remnant.

It was too heavy for me to carry. I started out with it in my arms, then tried shifting it over my shoulder, which was a mistake I'd probably remember in twenty years when I wondered what I'd done to my back.

When neither of those options worked, I dragged it. Dragging worked fine, except it left a heel furrow leading toward the driveway, which felt like a betrayal of the narrative we'd created, even if we were done filming. I changed direction and hauled it out the way Felix and I had come in the first evening, crossways through the orchard and over the cemetery's stone border, down to the edge of the pines. It didn't seem likely that anyone would chance on it during our final hours there.

Breakfast was a waffle party sponsored by a satisfied Ms. Tran. The owners had exceeded expectations. Alone in the dark on the last night, they had declared their intention to fix up the cemetery and the orchard once they'd finished the kitchen, before the bathroom. They hoped those repairs would bring peace to Han, appease him—which they had, since he was me, and I wouldn't be there to roll fog through their apple trees after we wrapped.

After breakfast, I returned to the site and dragged my figure the final yards through the ditch and out to the road. It weighed almost as much as me, but I managed to wrestle it into my little hatchback, where it fit diagonally across the bed if I flattened the rear seats. I unfolded my camping tarp to cover it; it only looked a little like a dead body. If anyone asked I could say it was firewood.

My bed was a welcome sight after a long night, but my head had just hit the pillow when Cath crashed through the door with her Bluetooth in her ear, talking on her phone about somebody on set who had pissed her off. "Oh, crap. Gotta go. My roommate is here asleep for some reason," she said, at a volume she did not lower in any way for the afore-mentioned roommate. I wasn't sure where she expected me to be, then I remembered I'd said I would camp on weekends. It hadn't really registered in my mind that I'd be finishing a night shoot and then going off somewhere. I desperately needed sleep.

I don't know why she'd bothered to get off the phone, when she wasn't any quieter without it. I dozed awhile longer as she proceeded to shower, then turn on her game console to start playing some shooting game, full volume. I got the message.

A quick web search told me there was a state park half an hour away. I stuffed some granola bars from the snack container into my backpack, along with my toiletries.

"See you Sunday," I said as the door closed. She didn't respond.

TRANSCRIPT
HAUNT SWEET HOME EPISODE 717—ACT I

Drone shot of JEREMY driving in Massachusetts. Medium shot of JEREMY turning onto a long drive- way framed by two stone pillars. Cut to JEREMY parking beside a blue electric Chevy. The Chevy has a bumper magnet reading "Don't Honk If You Love Librarians . . . They'll Shush You."

Cut to JEREMY walking up to the house and stop- ping to observe the exterior.

JEREMY
I'm here at Cleaveland House in western Massa- chusetts. Just from my first look, I can see why the Fergusons went for this place. Sometimes I get to these houses and the turrets look like they'll crumble in the wind, but this has been beautifully maintained, on the outside at least.

And those must be the Fergusons!

Cut to the couple standing awkwardly in front of their new house. CONOR is a handsome and hairy giant in baggy jeans, a long-sleeved rugby shirt, and a sweatband. MAGGIE is curvy, pretty, and pony-tailed, wearing well-fitting jeans and a black T-shirt that reads "The book was better."

                              JEREMY
Welcome to your new home! I know you must be
anxious to get inside, but first, can you tell
us a little more about yourselves?

                              MAGGIE
Our friends call us Beauty and the Beast.

                              JEREMY
Why?

                              MAGGIE
Because I love books and he's, well, furry, and
we've always told everyone we were going to
live in a castle someday, and now we have one
for real.

                              JEREMY
You sure do! Are you excited to go inside for
the first time as the official owners of your
very own castle?

                        MAGGIE and CONOR
Yes!

*Cut to interior hallway as the door opens. JER-
EMY, MAGGIE, and CONOR enter.*

                              JEREMY
Oh, wow.

                              MAGGIE
I know, right?

*JEREMY goes over to the ornate banister and
strokes it. CONOR wordlessly opens a built-in
grandfather clock and grins.*

                              JEREMY
This is amazing. You really did buy a castle.
This is straight out of a movie.

Cut to JEREMY, MAGGIE, and CONOR all taking semi-coordinated dance steps to a Time Warp-knockoff dance. The camera cuts away before they start the pelvic thrusts.

JEREMY
Okay, we all love the entryway. But what made you fall for the house?

MAGGIE
Walk this way.

Cut to MAGGIE affecting a funny walk, which JER-EMY and CONOR both imitate. They leave through a door on the left.

Cut to library. The library is not a huge room, but it is two stories tall. Some lower shelves are empty, but the upper ones have antique leather-bound books in them. There is a wrap-around balcony and a ladder on a rail. The room is filmed with warmth.

JEREMY
Wow, again. I know which movie you want to rec-reate in here. Care to do the honors?

Cut to MAGGIE, who grins and pushes off gently on the ladder, with one arm outstretched while fake Disney music plays.

JEREMY
And this was it? Love at first sight?

MAGGIE
Love at first sight.

JEREMY
And the former owners left books for you?

MAGGIE

Apparently, it was more trouble to deal with them than to include them with the house.

JEREMY

You said you're a librarian. Have you looked through them all already?

MAGGIE

Only a few shelves. I'm looking forward to cataloguing.

CONOR

After we tackle the renovations, of course.

MAGGIE (*sighing*)

Right, after.

JEREMY

That'll be a great reward for getting the hard stuff done. Who knows what's up there . . . I guess you'll find out! In the meantime, I could use a snack. How's the kitchen looking?

Cut to the kitchen, which is . . . drab. Claustrophobic, as filmed, much smaller than the library, with drop ceilings and bad light. The appliances are clunky and older, but not antique. Eighties, maybe. The wallpaper is brown and busy. Walnut cabinets add to the gloomy effect.

JEREMY

It's cleanish, at least.

JEREMY opens the refrigerator and closes it again without showing the interior.

JEREMY

I'm going to skip the snack. What are you planning on doing in here?

                    CONOR (*counting on his fingers*)
New appliances, lifted ceiling, better light-
ing, fresh paint, a new backsplash.

                         JEREMY
Sounds good, sounds good. What else is on this
floor?

*They peer into a tidy half bath, a dusty formal
dining room, a sitting room with unvarnished
hardwood flooring and good light.*

                         JEREMY
Do you know what happened in here? I get a bad
feeling in this room.

                         MAGGIE
Well, this is where the previous owner lived.

                         JEREMY
What do you mean?

                         CONOR
The last owner, Mrs. McGillicuddy, had health
problems. For the last twenty years of her life
she couldn't climb stairs, and the stairwell to
the second floor is too narrow for one of those
stairlift things. She had a hospital bed set
up in here, with all the natural light, and an
aide who stayed on a cot in the dining room to
be close. She was in here for a really long
time, with a TV and her books on tape—her eyes
were bad and she couldn't read her library anymore. Maggie hates that part.

                    MAGGIE (*looking genuinely upset*)
Can you imagine? Not that audiobooks aren't
great, but all those books going unread . . .

                    JEREMY
Did she die in here?

MAGGIE and CONOR nod.

                    JEREMY
And you say she wasn't able to go upstairs anymore? What's it like up there?

                    CONOR
Well, that's the other reason we got this place
at a price we could afford, I think.

*They climb the stairs. Cut to main bedroom.
There's a broken window and clear water damage
beneath it. The mattress on the carpet looks
like an animal has pulled stuffing out of it.
The carpet is stained and beige.*

                    JEREMY
Hmm. Something's been in here.

                    CONOR
Yeah, an exterminator is pretty high on the
priority list.

                    JEREMY
What else is on the priority list?

*MAGGIE points toward the bathroom. The bathroom
floor and walls are scummy. The toilet water is
black. The claw-foot bathtub has a thick ring.*

                    JEREMY
Ah. Yeah.

                    MAGGIE
If we're going to be living here while we work
on it, we definitely need to be able to shower.

                    JEREMY
How did Mrs. McGillicuddy shower?

Cut to the three principals standing behind the house, at an outdoor shower with a cement floor, a bench, and plastic walls.

MAGGIE
It's an option during summer, I guess.

Cut to upstairs, as we inspect two other bedrooms with peeling wallpaper and stained shag carpeting. A hall bathroom is also in awful shape. Cut to main bedroom.

JEREMY
I'm hearing you say the kitchen is a priority, and the exterminator, and the main bathroom, and the main bedroom. That's a lot of priorities.

CONOR
It's a lot of house.

JEREMY
But worth it?

MAGGIE
Worth it.

CONOR looks less sure.

JEREMY
Well, let's narrow down those priorities so you can get started on turning this house into the beauty we all know it can become . . . as long as there are no beasts around.

Cut to stuffing strewn around the mattress. Cut to an ominous shot of the library, as if something is lurking around the corner.

Cut to commercial.

4

My first month was an exhausting crash course in jump-and-do-it. Also, bats. After Stonemill Farm and its orchard, we filmed two Victorians on the main streets of nearby towns, then an off-season ski cabin an hour away. It meant our commute from the motel varied week to week, but I didn't mind beyond the gas money issue, which had improved after my first paycheck arrived.

On nights off, I camped on my own in the state park. I didn't really mind. The park was beautiful, with plenty of trails to explore. It probably would have been easier on my body to stick to my night schedule rather than boomeranging back and forth every weekend, but my tent heated up during the day, and skulking around the campsite in the dark seemed like it would be frowned upon. I learned to lean into the dreamy feeling brought by lack of sleep. The forest worked as a good punctuation mark on the weeks in any case; most houses didn't have grounds like Stonemill Farm's for me to escape into during the night, and solitude refreshed me for the next week of focusing on everybody's "hey, you" requests. I hiked and swam and napped and worked on my carving.

I was the weird camper the other campers avoided. The

other sites mostly housed RVs and trailers, or else multi-room family-sized tents. I set up my tiny thirdhand Boy Scout tent and sat at the picnic table facing my sculpture. Talking to it, sometimes, then sitting with it some more, always making absolutely certain before committing to the knife. On rainy days, the giant-tent families played board games and watched movies in their waterproofed living rooms, or packed up and drove home; I pulled my sculpture into my tent with me, or else leaned over the driver's seat to work on it in the car, fogging the windows and kinking my back.

The piece took shape. Balled fists dug into the figure's thighs. Turned-in shoulders; the isolation of being a friend-less feral sculptor at a family campsite. The face seemed beyond me, so I shaped planes, going for expressiveness over realism: a tension channeled up from those clenched fists and through the jaw. Frustration, aimless ambition, the conviction that everybody knew where they were going except for me. It wasn't a self-portrait, didn't look anything like me, but the more I worked on it, cut by tiny cut, weekend after weekend, the more it felt like a place I could put those thoughts so I didn't have to feel them alone.

On Sundays I packed up my campsite and covered the sculpture in the hatch again, reluctant to put it aside for the week, but curious to see what kind of place I'd be haunting next.

The fifth house came with a built-in story: the adjacent field had once grazed the famous Lennox cattle, before they were butchered and served at the restaurant across the street.

"Farm-to-table before farm-to-table was a thing," said

Andi at our planning meeting. I gave her a laugh, since nobody else did.

Felix frowned. "Farm-to-table isn't exactly an eerie concept."

"Think *Silence of the Lambs* for an aesthetic, minus the offensive villain," said Ms. Tran, which helped nobody. "The actual lamb part."

"Is there an actual lamb part in that movie?"

"Speaking of lamb, I see vindaloo coming."

Lulu arrived with our food. As she served me, she whispered, "Mara, when are you going to bring your cute cousin to my restaurant?"

She and her daughter both enjoyed the secondhand celebrity of serving us, and when I'd let slip that Jeremy and I were related, she'd made me promise to bring him to dinner sometime. I didn't think I'd actually catch him for a meal, but I agreed anyhow. If it turned out to be an overcommitment, she hopefully wouldn't realize I'd failed her until we were already gone.

I hadn't even caught a glimpse of him myself until our third site, because I was busy running around in the woods in the first week, and his night shoot the second week coincided with me driving to urgent care for a tetanus shot. The nail hadn't definitely been rusty, but it hadn't *not* been rusty, and the crawlspace was too dark to see for sure.

The third week's house was another Victorian. The owners played woodwinds in a local symphony, so we bought a twenty-dollar remote-controlled MP3 player to haunt them with the sounds of a sad violist. I was told to hide the speaker where they wouldn't find it and wouldn't even think to look, so while they were filming an interview in the kitchen, I climbed over the railing of the third-floor widow's walk, then shimmied on my butt across the peaked roof to the chimney. The machine barely made a sound falling into whatever debris had accumulated in the sealed-off fireplace; the owners would assume the music was coming from the walls.

As I turned to inch my way down, I noticed Jeremy on the sidewalk watching me. He made an exaggerated scream face with his hands on his cheeks when I caught his eye. I assumed that meant I'd finally get to say hey, but by the time I descended he was nowhere to be found.

"Is Jeremy filming tonight?" I asked Andi a little later.

She shook her head. "Not as far as I know."

"Weird," I said. "I saw him outside earlier."

"Oh, he might have just been walking around—this is the town he stays in. This nice old historic inn, a big step up from Ye Olde Mountainview. Why do you always ask about him?"

It had been almost a month, and I figured by then everyone knew I was a hard worker, so it wouldn't seem like nepotism anymore. Time to come clean. "He's my cousin."

"Huh! I'd never have known."

"Yeah, I know, not much of a resemblance."

"No," Andi said. "You're nice and you do everything we ask of you, and he's kind of a diva."

At the end of my shift, after remote-control conducting a viola concert through the hidden chimney, I sent him a DM. Hey, are we ever going to hang out this summer? The app said he had been active a minute before, but he didn't respond.

Now we were on our fifth shoot, and he and I still hadn't

chatted. It definitely felt like he was blowing me off. At least the job he'd offered me had existed. I just couldn't guarantee Lulu that he'd ever stop at her restaurant, or eat a single meal with me. I thought about asking through the parent grapevine if I'd done something to insult him, but I didn't think shaming him with the family would help.

Since then, I'd sent him only one more message: For someone who isn't haunting this show, you're doing a good job of ghosting me. No response.

The house next to the soon-to-be-haunted pasture had preceded the pioneering restaurant: a poorly maintained early-1800s build with a rotten front porch that looked like it was barfing sunflowers. Day crew's safety person said nobody was allowed to set foot on the porch, so we all had to use the mudroom entrance behind the kitchen. The screen door screeched and slammed behind everyone, despite copious applications of WD-40, making our comings and goings glaringly obvious. None of us were feeling this one.

We didn't *need* to do something different every time. There was no rule saying every haunting had to be unique. The early seasons had plenty of bones in the walls, partly because there often were bones in the walls. Squirrels, mostly, or snakes, or mice. That was before night crew started getting creative to keep the show fresh and interesting; before the fake hauntings began. Those early episodes were interesting enough on their own.

Even if sameness and stale concept hadn't threatened the show several seasons in, I think our night crew would have taken pride in finding the new—the haunted orchard, the ghostly viola. Hence Ms. Tran's excitement about the stupid pasture, even though the rest of us struggled to visualize it.

The house itself was boring, and so were its buyers, an accountant and an economics professor; we needed to liven things up. It was too soon to do spooky fog again, but it would have been impossible anyway, in a bare pasture surrounded by buildings. There was no way to plant anything with any subtlety, even in the middle of the night, with the streetlights positioned as they were. We didn't want to risk someone seeing us. So far, nobody had ever written an exposé, and everybody was hoping to keep it that way. Like with the owners, once the magic was ruined for the viewers it would be hard to bring it back.

"Hey," said Ms. Tran around eleven on the first night. "Hey" always meant me. "There's got to be someplace to hide. Go explore. In about half an hour, start making noises like Clarice would expect in this circumstance. Then wait some weird amount of time, not any expected interval, and do it again. Six cycles. Keep close enough to hear the screen door squeak, and if you hear it, clear out of wherever you are in case they come to look."

"Yes, ma'am," I said.

As I walked in the direction of the pasture, someone said, "Wait up!"

I turned. A slightly built white woman around my age came striding toward me from the direction of the house. "I'm Jo. I'm a floater—day sent me. Can I help with whatever you're doing?"

Annoyance flashed through me. Was I not getting my job done? I didn't need help. Still, she wore the uniform of our people—plain black T-shirt, black jeans—which meant she'd be able to hide as well as me. This was a team effort, and for the first time in my life I felt like part of a team. There was no reason to resent her. I tried to tamp it down.

"Sure," I said. "We need to find a hiding place from which to make tortured cow noises at random intervals for the next few hours."

"Hmm."

"Right? I don't know if there's any way to do it without sounding like people making cow noises, which is a really weird kind of haunting, and I think the owners will be on to us pretty fast. Also maybe, maybe I could handle *mournful* cow, but I'm happy to say I don't know what *screaming* cow sounds like. I'm a little afraid to look it up too, even if phones were allowed."

"I think I've got this. How about we split up, and you do your mournful cow noise, and I'll handle the scream?"

I eyed her again. The job had been assigned to me, but really I was just the only "hey, you" around. And I was definitely unsure about the screaming part. "I still haven't found one good place to hide, let alone two, is the only thing. Have you noticed any place?"

"Not near the pasture. Why don't you go behind the garage—there's a gap between the fence and the back wall. I'll go across the street behind the skimobile dealer. I think that's where the restaurant was. If we both start at the same time, our voices will come from two sides and bounce around so they can't tell it's people making the noise. Maybe."

It seemed as good a plan as any. I still hadn't messed up anything on this job too badly, and I didn't want to start now.

The backyard wasn't large. Some of it had been eaten by

a garage built to match the stone wall bordering the property, which in turn was built to look like the old stone walls that crisscrossed all the area forests and farms. You could tell both this garage and this wall were newer because they had actual mortar, and the stones were uniform. Funny since the house was one of the older ones we'd haunted; the town had ebbed and flowed around it.

Since everyone was using the house's rear door, I had to walk down the road to the next intersection, then double back behind through an overgrown lane. I crouch-walked the last fifty yards behind the low wall, then clambered over it to stand in the space between it and the garage. By then twenty minutes had passed, so I didn't have much time to kill. I spent the next ten minutes practicing my cow sound under my breath. The floater and I hadn't synchronized watches, so I had to trust that she and I would start our hauntings at more or less the same time.

At eleven thirty on the dot, I opened my mouth and started my best mournful cow imitation. At the same moment, something screamed. I didn't know if dying cows actually made that noise, but it was the most awful thing I'd ever heard in my life. Terrified, terrifying. As loud and close as if it were coming from inside my own head.

Through an open second-floor window, Felix's voice carried down. "What the fuck?" Normally they'd leave that kind of response to the owners, but I supposed it added to the authenticity if our crew members were unnerved too.

Other lights turned on in the house. They were probably headed to the windows overlooking the pasture. The sound ebbed, then came again. I realized I'd stopped making my sad cow noise; it was superfluous.

A second later, something skittered across my arm. A spider, maybe; I brushed it off gently, but I couldn't shake the feeling, and retreated toward the wall to escape it. The stone wall was smooth, so I leaned against it and closed my eyes. Still awake, not dozing, since at any point I might need to move if I heard someone leaving the house.

A little while later, Jo made her creepy noise again. It made the hairs on my arms stand up. I wished I could unhear it. The silence between screams made me appreciate silence like I never had before.

Thirty seconds into the third scream, another twenty-three minutes later, the screen door slammed. Hopefully Jo had the good sense to hide; I hadn't relayed to her the instruction about hiding if anyone left the house. I rolled off the wall and slipped around the garage to watch, figuring they'd be heading toward the pasture, and wouldn't look behind them to where I was following.

It was the two owners, both in matching Halloween-ghost pajamas they'd told us they'd bought for the occasion, trailed by Andi with a camera, Buzz with his boom mic, and Felix. Felix swiveled his head as he walked, like he was genuinely nervous. They went as far as the edge of the field, where Andi and Buzz recorded the couple holding on to the fence's top board like they were looking over a ship's deck and across turbulent seas. Even though I knew Jo was behind the skimobile sales place, when her sound came again it seemed to come from everywhere.

They strode toward the house so quickly I barely had time to duck behind the garage. We'd had four screams, not that I'd had anything to do with any but the first. I sat in my car through the fifth and sixth, wearing headphones in my best attempt to muffle the horrible sound. I should have been there, but she was doing a better job than me, so I figured it made sense for me to get out of the way and make sure I wasn't seen skulking around. After the sixth scream I set my alarm and closed my eyes; if I went back in I'd just draw attention to myself.

At breakfast, Ms. Tran was ecstatic. "I've never heard anything like that. I nearly peed my pants the first time you did it. Nice job!"

I nodded at the compliment. It was the most enthusiastic I'd ever seen her; I only wished I could take credit. If she asked me how I made the sound, I wouldn't have an answer. Was it okay to say that Jo had helped? She hadn't shown up at the end of the night, which I figured was the prerogative of a floating crew member. I cut my omelet in half—habit now—and dug in, willing Ms. Tran not to follow up. As I hoped, she moved on from the sound effect to the result.

"You should have seen them. I mean, you scared me too, and I was expecting it—they nearly jumped out of their skin the first time. And when they went to look and it sounded like your cow scream was coming from the grass itself, that was an amazing touch. I don't know how you did it. The fourth time, the husband cried. We may need to tone it down tonight if we don't want them to leave."

Felix said, "I told them about the acupuncturist I've been seeing on the weekends. I think they're going to try to book emergency treatments with her today. Hopefully that'll chill them out so we can scare them again. But damn, kid."

The praise warmed me until I remembered that I hadn't earned it.

"Can we get Jeremy in tonight?" Andi asked. "It would be cool to get a reaction shot from him without telling him what to expect."

Ms. Tran considered. "He'll probably hear about it during the day, so I don't think you'll get complete surprise, but it might still be worth it. I knew exactly when you were supposed to scream and it still scared the crap out of me. He'll be expecting some half-hearted 'moo' no matter what they describe."

Andi laughed. "If I ever start a country band, I'm calling it Some Half-Hearted Moo."

"I am mootiful, no matter what they say," crooned Felix.

The conversation devolved into an argument over whether that was a better band name or song name, indie or country. Buzz was silent as usual, until everyone else had let the conversation go, at which point he said, "Clear eyes, full heart, can't moos," and won the whole thing. Soon after, I asked for a to-go box for the second half of my breakfast, we paid our separate checks, and returned to the hotel. I collapsed into bed and tried to forget the full-hearted moo.

Forgetting didn't work; I heard it in my sleep. I dreamed it came from everywhere, unceasing. I was at home with my parents in their small, sunny kitchen. My mother was making coffee, and my father was burning toast, and they were both telling me what I should do with my summer vacation, even though I kept saying I had a job, and all the while, a horrible dying cow scream surrounded us. None of us paid it any attention, until my father went to the closet and grabbed the broom, and used the handle to knock on the ceiling.

The sound continued. He knocked on the door again—no, it had been the ceiling, but now it was coming from the door—and then Andi said, "Mara, wake up," and I fought my way up from the dream to realize she was pounding on the door for real. My motel room was full of smoke and the fire alarm was blaring.

Outside the darkened room the noon-bright sun shocked my eyes. I shielded them to see the rest of the night crew standing around in their sleeping clothes—Felix wore only a pair of gold briefs, which I couldn't unsee. The motel employees were gathered around my door waiting on Andi's knock. Valentina, the head housekeeper, had a key out, which I guess she would have used in a second if I hadn't answered. Even Lulu and Sathya and their restaurant staff stood outside the kitchen door watching. A fire engine clanged in the distance.

The motel manager pushed past me into my smoky room. He emerged a minute later with a towel wrapped around his hand, holding a blackened saucepan. "Hot plate was left on," he said.

The hollow, four-hours-sleep eyes of my crewmates all turned my way.

"It's not mine," I said. "We had breakfast and I went straight to bed. My roommate must have left it on."

I tried to remember if anything had been out of the ordinary. Like usual, the room had been dark and empty when I arrived back in the early dawn. I took a shower instead of crashing immediately, only because I'd never shaken the cobwebby feeling from behind the garage. I didn't remember seeing a red light on the hot plate, or smelling anything.

"My roommate's," I repeated.

The manager turned to Ms. Tran. "Hot plates are against the motel rules."

"I'll tell the day producer to tell her staff; mine wouldn't make that mistake. I promise it won't happen again." Ms. Tran's gaze lingered on me. I wondered if I was about to be fired, or if I had gotten Cath fired, and if I was a jerk for repeating "my roommate," but she didn't say anything else.

The fire truck screamed up a minute later. Three fire-fighters crowded in and emerged with the hot plate. After that, the alarm quieted, and the onlookers dispersed. My room, unfortunately, smelled like smoke and burnt food. I threw my backpack in my car and hid Cath's game console under her comforter, then left the door open. Hopefully she didn't have anything else someone might bother stealing while our space aired out.

I tried sleeping in my car in front of the room so I could keep an eye on it, but with the backseats folded down and the sculpture under the tarp, I couldn't recline the front seat to stretch out. Finally, I dragged my smoky pillow and blanket to the pool area and passed out in a lounge chair. Across the street, a bell dinged every time someone pulled up at the gas pumps, and beyond, the highway roared.

I managed a fitful three hours. No more screaming, no more dreams, but little of what could actually be called sleep. Eventually, it became too hot under the blanket. I pushed it off and slid into the pool in my sleeping clothes. I sank to the bottom and held my breath for a minute, then pushed toward the surface. At least I could be refreshed, if not rested.

The room and everything in it still smelled. I showered again and put on clean, but smoky clothes. I reconnected

Cath's game console so her first thought wouldn't be panic, left her a note that hopefully sounded more explanatory than accusatory, locked the door, and dragged my weary body over to Lulu's.

Felix wrinkled his nose when I sat down next to him.

"I know," I said. "You don't have to say it. I'll wash all my clothes as soon as I get a chance."

Jeremy arrived punctually at 10:30 P.M. We were sitting around the backyard picnic table, giving the owners a few minutes of privacy before our next incursion. The couple—Paul and Marta—had gone inside to get ready for bed after a long day of shooting, during which they'd retiled the bathroom floors. I'd helped Aunt Bea lay flooring once, and I remembered aching by the end of it, at half their age. According to their interviews they were sore and exhausted and ready for an early night: a perfect time for Jeremy to pop in for a chat.

He greeted the other crew members before turning to me as if he hadn't blown me off for five weeks. His hair was carefully styled, and he already had makeup on. He wore expensive-looking black jeans and an equally expensive low V-neck that exposed a large swath of his model chest.

"Mara! How's it going? You look like they're running you ragged. And why do you smell like smoke?"

Everyone looked over like they were surprised he knew the PA's name. I had only told Andi and Lulu he was my cousin, and I guess neither of them had told anyone else.

"My roommate accidentally started a fire today, so I didn't sleep. Otherwise, I'm good. How's your summer going?" It was the closest I could get to a dig about the fact that this was our first conversation since I'd started the job, given how everyone else was watching with interest.

"Good. No complaints here. Everybody on this crew is so professional—they make the job easy."

He flashed a smile at the small audience, then turned to talk privately with Ms. Tran.

"Suck-up," I muttered, not hiding my annoyance. I'd gotten the message that he didn't want to be around me, and that he didn't want people to know we were related, but I wasn't sure what I had done to deserve to be treated like a casual acquaintance. If he hadn't wanted me here, why had he gotten me the job? Given all that, if he was going to play it cool, so would I. Mostly.

My crewmates headed inside to where their equipment was already set up. The plan was to film the couple drinking tea at the kitchen island, and for Jeremy to knock on the door as if he'd stopped in for a friendly visit. Then they'd offer Jeremy tea, and talk about their day some more as if he hadn't just spent it renovating with them, and then they'd all hear a scream. The owners and Jeremy knew about the tea-and-conversation part, but not the scream, though anyone who'd watched the show would have a guess as to what would happen next based on what had happened the night before.

My job was to make the cow sound again, so I was left outside. I'd head over to the skimobile place in a minute, since it obviously had better acoustics than the place I'd hidden. I sat at the picnic table wondering how to duplicate the sound Jo had made, and kicking myself for not having recorded her.

I was trying to remember if it was more of a scream or a moan, when Jo walked around the corner of the house. "Hey—I heard you might need help again. Last night was fun. I don't usually get to do stuff like that."

"Not too many people do," I said. "Privilege of my position."

"Ah, yes. The overwhelming privilege of the production assistant. What's the plan?"

"Basically the same as last night, but only twice. Once about ten minutes from now. Jeremy's here, and we're hoping your cow sound will scare him as well as the couple. Then again sixteen or seventeen minutes later. Not fifteen, not an interval they might think they could count. Then he'll leave, and the owners will be up all night waiting for the third time."

"Aye, captain. Can do." Jo saluted, then sauntered toward the road. I should have asked her how she screamed like that, and if I could record it. I could always record and then ask permission later. We'd all signed waivers about how everything we said and did on the job could be used, so her dying cow technically fell under those permissions.

My phone would still get me in trouble, but I knew Buzz usually kept his little recorder in his van, which was parked up the road. I was rummaging for the recorder by the light of the lone streetlamp when the sound started. It was just as horrific as the night before, even when I expected it. Like an actual cow screaming in terror, a sound I wouldn't have thought I could name so specifically, but hearing it, that felt like exactly the right description. The noise stopped, and there was silence for a moment, then the screen door creaked open. I stayed put, afraid to call attention to myself by exiting the van.

It wasn't hard to tell where the group was: the agitated voices carried. They were by the pasture when Jo made the sound for the second time. By then I'd found the recorder, but I still couldn't leave. I hit the red button anyway; even this far away, it was as loud as if she were in the vehicle with me.

I waited until the noise stopped, and then until I heard the door hinges again, before I slipped from the van. On my way out, I grabbed a flat of water, my usual way of being the person beneath notice if any homeowners ever looked out a window when they weren't supposed to.

I'd just reached the picnic table when Andi and Buzz rushed out the door with their equipment and swung around to face the house. They were followed a moment later by the couple, who had both thrown jackets over their pajamas. Marta carried a small bag, and Paul had a wallet and keys in one hand and a phone to his ear with the other. Jeremy followed.

"—not right," Marta was saying. "We've been vegan for fourteen years. I don't wear leather. I don't deserve to be haunted by cows."

Jeremy wore his well-practiced sympathy/concern face; I'd seen it on the show a number of times, though it wasn't part of his personality around family at all. "It's probably not about you, if you think about the history of this place. Maybe they're asking you for help, not haunting you."

"What are we supposed to do? How is fixing up this house going to help them?"

"Have you considered starting a livestock sanctuary?" Jeremy was trying hard to win them back. "Stay through the night, and we can talk about it again in the morning. It's late to go anywhere."

The man held up his keys. "We're going to Motel 7. We heard that scream six times last night, and I want to be gone before I have to hear it again. We can talk about it tomorrow, but right now I'm feeling like I don't want to set foot on this property ever again. It's too much."

The crew filmed the couple driving away, then Andi and Buzz jumped in the van and followed, leaving Jeremy, Ms. Tran, and Felix standing in the backyard under the harsh glare of the porch light.

Jeremy turned to Ms. Tran. "What was that? I've never heard anything like it. You could have warned me."

"You knew it was coming. It's not my fault you got scared."

"I nearly pissed myself. I want to approve that footage before you include it."

"Not going to happen; get yourself a producer credit if you want oversight. You didn't do anything embarrassing, and we won't do anything to harm your image. Relax. Take some deep breaths, then follow them and change their minds."

"You heard. They said they're done for the night, and I am too. We can work on convincing them tomorrow morning." He stalked over to his car and drove away in the opposite direction of the others. Interesting to see how little clout he had; not enough to bully Ms. Tran, certainly.

When Jeremy was gone, Felix turned to Ms. Tran. "Well, that went well."

She sighed. "Vegans. Cow screams might have been a little much, given that extenuating circumstance."

"It's their fault they bought a place with this history," Felix said. "Not our fault for using it. But we should probably follow."

Ms. Tran nodded in agreement and the two of them walked off without ever looking in my direction. I wasn't sure what I was supposed to do: Follow as well? Stay put for when they returned?

Heading down the road after them seemed like the proactive choice, but nobody had locked up, and I wasn't sure what needed protecting; the day equipment, at the very least. And I was tired, as tired as I'd been since the first week. I put my head on my arms on the picnic table and closed my eyes. I'd wake up when I heard the van return, or voices coming around the house.

The voice that woke me was Cath's, not one of my own crew. "I guess it's not sleeping on the job if your shift is over."

I opened my eyes to a predawn wash, and a couple of day folks looking at me curiously.

"They didn't come back," I said, meaning the night crew.

Cath thought I meant the owners. "Yeah—I hear they're heading home to Amherst or wherever they're from. Kalima and Ms. Tran both spent all night at some motel trying to talk them out of it, but they're done. Reselling-the-house done. Do you know what happened?"

I remembered the expressions on their faces; they looked like people who had made up their minds.

"Something must have scared them real bad," Cath continued, clearly hoping for details.

"Must have," I said, shrugging. Andi had said never to talk to day about what we did at night. "So what happens now if they won't continue?"

"We'll film Jeremy talking about their decision and what happened, and then we'll do some more interior stuff without them. It'll be spliced together in editing. We always film way more than we need, so I'm sure we've got enough footage already to cobble together an episode."

"Even without their participation?" I asked. "At their house?"

"Sure. They've already signed everything. The contract says we can be here when they aren't, even if they aren't participating anymore. We can still use what we've got. And meanwhile we might get a long weekend! I'll get some extra time to air out our room. I left some quarters for you to wash your smoky stuff."

"Thanks," I said. It was the nicest thing she'd said to me yet. The quarters were kind of an apology, even if "I'll get some extra time" made it clear as usual that I'd have to find someplace else to be for the weekend, even a long one.

TRANSCRIPT
HAUNT SWEET HOME EPISODE 717—ACT II

JEREMY *(voiceover, over shots of the exterior, then various rooms)*

I'm here in western Massachusetts with Maggie and Conor Ferguson, who have bought their dream house, with their dream library. They have their work cut out for them, though, between the dingy, outdated kitchen, the neglected second floor, and the biohazard main bathroom. They've spent their first day cataloguing the issues and prioritizing, so now comes the big question.

Cut to JEREMY and FERGUSONS eating pizza over the kitchen counter.

JEREMY
Have you decided where you're going to sleep tonight?

MAGGIE
I think we should sleep in the library. It feels cozy and safe to me.

CONOR
I think we should sleep in the drawing room where the old lady slept. It's closer to the bathroom, and we haven't checked if those high shelves are stable.

JEREMY
Any votes for the second floor?

                    MAGGIE and CONOR
No.

                         MAGGIE
Why would the shelves be unstable? The house
was inspected.

                         CONOR
The inspector looked at the house, not the
furniture. Besides, how long do you think it's
been since those upper shelves were dusted? The
drawing room is way cleaner. My asthma . . .

                         MAGGIE
Fine. I suppose I'll have the rest of my life
to fall asleep surrounded by my books.

                         JEREMY
That's the spirit! Marriage is all about com-
promise. Let's get you situated in the drawing
room. Hey, did your old apartment have a drawing room?

                         MAGGIE
It didn't!

*Shots of the couple inflating an air mattress in
the drawing room and setting up a lamp beside
it, of the couple taking turns brushing their
teeth in the small hallway bathroom, of CONOR
braving an outdoor shower with trunks on. Cut
to the three standing in the vestibule.*

                         JEREMY
Well, the drawing room looks nice and cozy. I'm
going to let you get some rest, and I'll be back
bright and early to get started on the—

            CONOR   MAGGIE
            Kitchen.   Bathroom.

JEREMY

Right. It's gonna be a busy week. Good night!
Sleep tight! Don't let whatever was in the mattress upstairs bite.

*Shot from exterior into drawing room, of CONOR
and MAGGIE tucking into bed. CONOR picks up a
tablet and MAGGIE picks up an enormous leather-
bound book.*

Exterior, night, beside Jeremy's car.

JEREMY

With Conor and Maggie doing a little light
reading before bed, I'm going to take the opportunity to head out. Whatever we start on
tomorrow, we're going to need a full night of
sleep. Hopefully we'll all get it.

*Distant shot of Jeremy's car heading out be-
tween the two gate pillars. Camera pulls back
slowly and turns around so it's facing the
drawing room window again, as MAGGIE puts down
her book and turns off the lamp. The camera
stays on the darkened window for a long beat.
Then there's a heavy thud.*

CONOR

What the [censored] was that?

Cut to commercial.

5

I checked my messages as I walked to the car. There wasn't even a WHERE ARE YOU? Which meant I'd probably made the right decision in staying at the house, even if I fell asleep. I drove to our breakfast spot to catch the morning breakdown, but nobody was there.

I DIDN'T MEAN TO MISS THE MEETING, I texted Andi. AM I IN TROUBLE?

IT'S OK, she responded after a minute. WE FIGURED YOU WERE WATCHING THE LOCATION SINCE NOBODY HAD LOCKED UP.

Then, WE'VE GOT THE REST OF THE WEEK OFF! WHAT-CHA GONNA DO?

I wondered if someone was supposed to tell me officially to take off, or if it was okay to hear it secondhand. NOT SURE, I responded.

I'M HEADING TO NYC, she wrote. DYING FOR GOOD SUSHI.

Was it an invitation? If I asked to tag along, she could always say no. I didn't know anyone in the city, though, so I'd end up spending money on hotels on a weekend where I was losing two days of pay. And what if she said no, she was meeting other friends, better friends, real friends? What if

I made it awkward and she stopped chatting with me, and I became "hey, you" even to her?

Not worth it. HAVE FUN IN NYC! I MIGHT GO CHECK ON MY GRANDMA AND DO SOME FREE LAUNDRY. It would have been nice to have been invited to New York, to know my presence was a welcome one, but the more I thought about it, the more a weekend of not-camping appealed; I was more tired than I wanted to admit.

Nobody officially told me to go home, but I watched and waved as the other night folks drove away, and finally tossed my garbage bag of smoky clothes onto my tarp-covered carving. I slipped behind the wheel and was about to start the car when I realized my eyes were closed. I wasn't going to make it anywhere without more sleep. There was no rush, anyway, beyond trying not to cross paths with Cath, who was still working; might as well nap in my own smelly bed.

I stirred as the afternoon sun angled through the gap between the curtain and the window in a single beam concentrated on my pillow. I felt a thousand times better.

When I opened the door, the sun hit me even more directly. The only sounds were trucks on the highway and a Spanish pop station blaring from a radio on Valentina's cart. Mine was the only car down the row.

"I'm not usually here in the afternoons," someone said. "Is it always this quiet?"

I shaded my eyes and Jo came into view. "It's pretty mellow during the day. Did they let you all off early for the weekend too?"

She nodded. "I'm the first wave. Snuck out early without helping to pack up, but nobody's going to miss me."

The thought of still being here when the day crew returned was a good argument for moving on. I grabbed my bag, locked the door, and made it to my car before I turned again to where Jo was still standing.

"Hey, this is random, but do you want to come with me? I'm going to my grandmother's house, which sounds boring, but she's an artist, and her house is full of cool stuff, and she's in Taos this month, so you won't be stuck hanging out with somebody's grandma. It's a three-hour drive to someplace even more in the middle of nowhere than here, but it beats staying here for a long weekend."

Once I'd started the pitch I felt like I had to commit to it. Jo seemed cool enough. The summer I'd worked at Girl Scout camp all I'd wanted was to be invited when the other staff hung out together, went to Philly or New York or an amusement park. Maybe I should have tried making the invitation myself; at least I'd have known where I stood.

For a moment she looked like she was making a mental calculation, and I thought she was going to turn me down and force me to spend my whole drive replaying the conversation to figure out how much of a fool I'd made of myself. But then she said, "Why not? You're right; it beats staying here."

"Cool." I tried not to sound overeager. "It'll be nice to have company on the drive. How long do you need to get ready?"

"Have backpack, will travel." She pointed to her shoulder. I hadn't noticed she was carrying a bag. It was the same faded black as her T-shirt.

Normally, conversation with a total stranger would be awkward, but she was a stranger who worked more or less the same job as me, at the same workplace, and it was fun comparing notes on the different owners and houses and stuff. If nothing else, we could be friends on the basis of her imitation of my cousin Jeremy hearing a scary cow.

We made it to Oma's in early evening. There were a few reasons I chose my grandmother's house over my parents', starting with the fact that I didn't have a room at the latter anymore. When I'd moved into AJ's apartment building near the community college a few years before, it was because they'd suggested we separate our finances for the purposes of financial aid; I wouldn't have minded staying home to save money, but they had insisted it was important for me. The second I moved out, they walled off my room and bathroom, added a kitchenette, and threw it onto a short-term rental site.

It wasn't like there was any reason for them to keep my childhood bedroom intact with me living ten miles away. Maybe their faith that I wouldn't bounce back into their house was reassuring; at the same time, I couldn't help thinking they might have left the safety net up a little longer rather than making it a literal impossibility for me to return, like pushing a fledgling from a nest.

With my apartment sublet to another BrewHaHa server, this was the first time I'd had to consider where to stay; I'd decided on Oma's grandkid crash pad, comfortably unchanged in my lifetime, rather than the pullout couch in my parents' living room. I supposed I could've checked if the rental room was available, but that made me feel even more pathetic. Anyway, staying at Oma's didn't make me feel like I was settling. She had always said that we and our friends were welcome there.

I pointed out her old shop by the road as we turned into the driveway. It had been years now since she'd sold the last pieces and closed it up, but she still insisted someone paint the exterior every summer—one of her kids, or one of their kids. My turn had come two years before, and I'd used a dusky purple called Concordance, with cornflower trim; the next year my cousin Greg had yelled at me for choosing paint so dark he'd needed three coats of primer to cover it. In the twilight, I couldn't quite tell what colors had been selected this time, but its bright trim stood out against the approaching night.

We continued up toward what looked deceptively like a small ranch house from the front, perched as it was on top of the hill. I parked by the front door and we walked around to the rear.

"Whoa," Jo said. "That's a lot of ducks."

"One hundred and sixty-six, to be exact. All the known Anseriformes, including ducks and geese and swans. I tried to memorize them all as a kid, but I think I've forgotten a bunch."

Wooden birds lined the railings and the deck, every one of them different. Oma had made them for a climate-change show at the Whitney years before; every day she'd taken one away, until at the end of the exhibit there were none in the room. Some art collector would probably have paid a million bucks for the lot, but she brought them home to get beaten up by the weather like so many hunting decoys.

The key was kept under a duck whose beak had broken off; I couldn't remember which cousin had taken the blame, but the rest of us thought it might have been on purpose, since before the de-beaking we'd been forced to remember it by counting forty-three from the door and hoping nobody had switched it, or else trying to remember what a bufflehead looked like as distinguished from a lesser scaup and a redhead and a mallard.

As usual, when I opened the door the scent of mineral oil hit first—the smells of mineral oil and wood were inextricable from this house. Stairs led up and down from the back door; we went up first, since I was eager to show off Oma's work.

Even though she had her store and fine-art sales, she'd kept a fair number of pieces (see, for example, the ducks). She never explained why, but as she finished each, she had either taken it down the hill to her shop, or to her living room. Where other grandmothers had china cabinets and doll collections, every inch of her floor and cabinet space was taken up by her sculptures.

No ducks inside. These were the abstracts, the life-size, the personal pieces. The things museums occasionally begged her for, and she occasionally loaned, or else said, "Maybe when I'm dead, if the family doesn't want them." As a kid, I played hide-and-seek among them, and dressed the most humanlike forms, and put on shows for a frozen audience, pretending they were members of the family that had more time for me.

I tried to gauge Jo's reaction as she took it all in. She walked among the carvings, occasionally stroking a silken curve. No museum reverence; Oma would approve.

"These are beautiful," she said after she'd explored the entire room. "Your grandmother is so skilled. Is that where you get it from?"

Not the response I'd expected. "Sorry?"

"The sculpture under the tarp in your car. I peeked when you stopped for gas. It looked too much like a body, so I had to check. I'm assuming you carved it? It's not finished, and the style is different from these."

For a second I felt exposed, intruded upon. Her explanation made sense, though. If I were traveling with a stranger and thought there was a body in the backseat, I'd probably peek too. I tried to laugh it off. "Yeah, that's mine. Definitely not finished."

"Are you going to show it to her?"

"Maybe someday. If I get to a point where I'm happy with it. You can see it's got to clear a high bar." I waved at the sculptures around us.

I pointed out a few of my favorites, then we headed downstairs to the Grandchild Zone. The Grandchild Zone was a large basement rec room with two narrow dorm rooms off of it, each with three bunk beds. They'd originally been named Boys and Girls but had been relabeled Pine and Maple when my cousin Roan came out as nonbinary. Among ourselves we'd always just called them Loud and Quiet, and divided up according to who tolerated late-night talkers. I always got sent to Quiet because they said I was too young to stay up.

"You can have Maple and I'll sleep in Pine; there won't be anyone else here this weekend. Pick any bed except the last one on the top—nobody's gotten around to fixing the broken slats. The bathroom is two doors down." I opened the closet and grabbed two sets of sheets, *Jurassic Park* and *Little Mermaid*. "You choose. If you want a second pillow, just grab one off another bed."

She reached for the *Little Mermaid* sheets and went to make her bed. I put dinosaurs on mine, took my laundry down the hall to the washing machine, then returned to the rec room and threw myself into the enormous black beanbag we'd always called Darth Vader. Jo emerged from Maple/Quiet a moment later.

"Just so you know, I'm a little anxious about making sure you're happy you came with me." I had decided to be frank. "There are fewer food options than near the motel, and nothing's as good as Lulu's. We can get some groceries and cook upstairs if we want. There's a decent coffee shop slash comedy club, but I bailed on my job there to take this one, so I don't really want to show my face. We can go to a movie, or swim at the lake if you're into swimming, and my extended family has these big bonfires on Saturday nights if you want to brave a family thing."

She settled into the yellow beanbag, Big Bird. "One: Don't worry about entertaining me. You warned me before we left that this wasn't excitement central, and frankly, a quiet weekend sounds wonderful. Two: A movie sounds great, or a hike. Three: Family bonfire sounds fantastic, after a good night's sleep. Honestly, right now I just want to pass out."

Once she'd said it, I realized I was exhausted again. "Are you sure you don't mind crashing at nine?"

"My body is so confused at this point. I don't care what time it is. I just want to close my eyes and sleep until I wake up without an alarm. Those bunk rooms with no windows look glorious. You can get back to anxiously trying to entertain me tomorrow."

I grinned. "Deal."

We spent the next two days seeing all the sights of exciting northeast nowhere. We did a little hiking, and binge-watched our own show instead of going to the movies. She had a lot of questions about the area, and my family, so she would know who was who at the bonfire on Saturday night. We slept at night and soaked in as much sunlight as we could, given my current employ.

By the time we made it down the road to AJ's, my father and his sisters were already deep in song in front of the roaring fire, along with two cousins—a couple of guitars, a couple of fiddles, banjo. The fourth sibling, AJ, had the grill down and was poking at the dark shapes on it. As we walked toward them, I realized I'd never brought anyone here with me before.

I turned to Jo. "They can be really direct. I apologize if they give you a hard time."

"Enough warnings," she replied.

My mother sat in the grandfather chair; some people insisted on their own chair every time, but she never cared. She sat beside my father and his fiddle, slapping time against her knee, since she always said she loved music too much to play it herself, even though she was a decent guitarist. I felt kind of similarly, always self-conscious around my talented, well-practiced family. It was a silly thing. I touched both parents on a shoulder as we passed, ducking to avoid my father's bow.

My mother twisted in her seat. "Mara! We didn't expect to see you this summer. Did something happen?"

Heat rose in my face. Did I get fired, she meant. "No. The job is going great. They gave us a long weekend is all."

I introduced Jo, trying to let the insult go. The story my family told about me was the product of their own editing, and like an episode of *Haunt Sweet Home*, it had only a tangential relationship to actual fact.

We pulled up a couple of empty thrones to listen. I took Jeremy's, since he definitely wouldn't be making an appearance. It wasn't a cold night, but the fire felt good, and I leaned into the warmth. Jo examined the throne she had chosen, another cousin's, with a thicket of vines carved up the back. "These chairs. More of your grandmother's work?"

I nodded. "They're not sitting in their right thrones tonight. There's one for each of my dad's siblings and their spouses, and for all their kids except me."

"Except you?"

"She wouldn't do it until you were twenty, because she said she had no clue who you were until then. But her hands got bad when I was a teenager and she never made mine. The first few started out as dining room furniture in the house we're staying at—when my dad and his siblings were kids—but when his brother AJ got married and built this fire pit Oma brought the thrones here as a wedding present. Except it was a fiasco, because what kind of present is six special chairs for six family members when a seventh person is joining the family? Aunt Carmen said Oma should have made another for her, and Oma said she hadn't yet found the right piece of wood. Except she never did find one, and it's possible she always knew they'd split. It was a sore spot through the entire marriage. Which is probably more than you needed to know . . ."

"Probably," Jo agreed, grinning.

The musicians took a break for food after a few songs. I speared two hot dogs and put them in buns and handed the second one to Jo on a paper plate. "Condiments and chips on the table. There's this weird fruit ketchup my uncle

Jacques makes. I know that sounds strange, but it's really good. Some Quebecois thing."

I went to grab a drink from the cooler. When I returned, her plate had disappeared and she was chatting with my father, who, a moment later, held his fiddle and bow out to her. She looked like she was concentrating very hard as she put it to her chin and played a couple of halting notes, then a sprightly melody I didn't recognize. Everyone turned to look, and when she finished there was a smattering of applause.

One of my cousins went into the house and emerged with another fiddle, and Jo handed my father's back to him. The new one wasn't as good as his, somebody's school in-strument, I think, but it wasn't awful, and she played it well. When the music started up again, they let her into the players' circle, leaving me to stare at the fire. I tried to tamp down my jealousy; if I'd wanted to learn an instrument, I could have.

At the next break, I nudged her. "We should go."

She looked over as if she'd forgotten I existed. "Can't we stay a little longer? This is fun."

"I'm ready to crash. Tomorrow's a long day for me." The truth, if only part of it. "Maybe somebody can give you a ride if you want to stay longer?"

She sighed and reluctantly nestled the borrowed fiddle into its case. When we left, everyone hugged her goodbye as if they had known her forever.

"Come home with Mara anytime," my mother told her.

She was smiling when she slipped into the passenger seat beside me. I held in my annoyance long enough to turn the car around in the crowded driveway; it spilled out before we even reached the road. "You didn't say you played fiddle."

"You didn't ask."

"It might've come up when I told you they all played instruments."

"Why?" From the corner of my eye, I saw the smile fall from her face. "You were talking about them, not me. I didn't expect them to play stuff I was familiar with. And I wouldn't have said anything if your father hadn't offered his fiddle. Are you mad at me?"

"No." Yes. I wasn't sure what I was upset about. Not her playing my father's fiddle, not exactly; what bothered me was the point of connection. The fact that he chatted with her about music, but when he turned to me it was to ask if I'd be trying to make school happen again in the fall. "Make school happen," like it was my fault it hadn't happened yet, which it was, but that didn't mean he got to say it. The fact that I'd overheard her telling one of my cousins about my weird roommate as if it were her story to tell. Such a funny jealousy. I'd invited her, promised her my family was cool, and now I was angry that they'd gotten along.

I tried again. "It's just . . . you play the same music they play, you chatted with them like you'd known them forever. They didn't give you a hard time about working at this job, because of course they didn't; why would they give you a hard time? They didn't ask you if it was temporary. And at the cow place you scared the owners better than I did."

"I'm sorry. I was just trying to get along with everybody. And to help you, at the cow pasture. Did you not want help?"

"I did. I just didn't expect you to be so good at it. Look,

this is all in my head. This is going to sound silly, and I know I'm being completely unreasonable, but right this moment it feels like you're better at being me than I am. Does that sound stupid?"

She looked out her window. "It doesn't sound stupid. I didn't mean to be better at being you. It's not my fault you're bad at it."

"Wait, what?" If I hadn't misheard her, it was an epically shitty thing to say.

"Your life is amazing. Great family, an interesting job you turn out to be good at, the freedom to try whatever you want, and you're just going through the motions, like none of it is worth anything. Have you ever considered appreciating what you have? Waking up and saying, 'How cool that my life has brought me to this moment'?"

My hands tightened on the steering wheel. "How is this any of your business? We aren't good enough friends for you to give me shit."

"Is anybody? Who are your friends? Your cousins barely said hi to you."

"They're older than me. We never had a chance to become friends."

"Sure, maybe."

"I'm sorry I brought you here," I said. "And I'm sorry I let you help out. Your screamy cow was so scary you ruined the shoot."

Her eyes flashed in the dark. "That was nothing. I'll show you scary. I hope you didn't like this job too much—oh yeah, I forgot, you don't like anything too much. It makes it easier not to care when you lose it."

I turned up the hill at Oma's little shop, and didn't say

anything as I parked. I was blinking back tears, some omni-directional combination of hurt and anger. This was a lesson in not bringing home strangers, even if you worked with them and thought they might be cool.

"I'm tired," I said. "I'm going to bed, and in the morning we'll drive to the motel, and we can go back to not being friends."

"Are you sure that's what you want?" Her tone was different now. I didn't know her well enough to read it.

"You said it yourself. I don't like anything too much." It was a lousy end to a good weekend, and I felt even worse for recognizing that I had caused it. I didn't know how to fix it, and my mouth kept making it worse. I didn't hear her behind me as I walked around the house. When she still hadn't come in by the time I'd brushed my teeth, I locked the door to Pine, climbed into my bunk, and closed my eyes.

I woke in the middle of the night to find Jo standing next to my bed.

"This isn't how I wanted it to be," she said sorrowfully. The room was dark, but I could see her face; she looked like me. "We're in this together."

"I know. I don't know why I'm like this." I put a hand out to her—I'm not sure what I was going to do, shake her hand, or squeeze it, but it passed through her. Then I remembered the locked bedroom door, and glanced over; it was closed. When I looked again, she was gone.

She wasn't around in the morning. Not in the Maple bunk room, not in the beanbags, not upstairs. My car was locked, and I couldn't remember if I'd locked it or left it with her still sitting in it. I texted Andi to see if she had a cell number for Jo, and she responded, WHICH JO? and I realized I didn't know her last name.

I made breakfast and waited awhile, but she didn't show up, even though she had to know we were supposed to be on site by 4 P.M. to set up the next house before the owners arrived in the morning. I waited as long as I could, trying to think of a way to contact her without contact info. I wrote a note to Oma, thanking her for the crash space. Then a note to Jo that I put in an envelope at the door, in case she returned, which hopefully my grandmother wouldn't read, since it basically said I had ditched someone at her house. Then a PS added to Oma's note saying I'd made something I wanted to show her the next time I came home.

Finally, I'd run out of buffer time and excuses not to leave. I was the ass who'd picked a fight with my—friend? Coworker?—and abandoned her across state lines, three hours away. How nice to have a new addition to all the ways I was a lousy person. I still didn't know if she'd left the night before—her appearance in my locked bedroom seemed more and more like a dream—or that day, or if she'd called a super-expensive rideshare or had a friend pick her up. Hell, maybe my father or one of my cousins had come and gotten her. She was an adult. She wasn't my responsibility.

TRANSCRIPT
HAUNT SWEET HOME EPISODE 717—ACT III

Exterior shot of darkened drawing room window. Loud thud. Voices inside.

> CONOR

What the [censored] was that?

> MAGGIE

Maybe fruit falling on the car? There's a black walnut tree by the car park.

> CONOR

It came from inside the house.

> MAGGIE

That's such a horror movie thing to say.

> CONOR

But it did! You didn't hear it like it was across the hall?

> MAGGIE

Across the hall is my library.

> CONOR

Yes. I think it came from your library.

> MAGGIE

I was fine with a haunted bedroom or bathroom. I don't want a haunted library.

> CONOR

There's no such thing as ghosts. A book fell, or whatever was living in the mattress got into

there. We should probably go let it out before
it does any damage.

                    MAGGIE
Yeah, you're right.

*The lamp turns on. We are still looking through
the window as the couple get out of bed.*

*Cut to the couple in the dark hallway, followed
by a handheld camera. MAGGIE enters first and
kicks something in the darkness.*

                    MAGGIE
Where's the light switch?

*CONOR turns on a pocket flashlight, and uses it
to find the switch. They enter the room to find
a hardcover book laying open on the floor—that's
what MAGGIE kicked. The camera has circled to
film them in the doorway.*

                    MAGGIE
It couldn't have fallen there.

                    CONOR
Not even from up high? If it fell from way up
high it could have bounced over to the door. Or
slid or something.

                    MAGGIE
Maybe . . .

*CONOR picks up the book. He looks at the cover
and startles.*

                    MAGGIE
What book is it?

                    CONOR
I thought you said this was a law library?

MAGGIE

Yes, most of what they left are old Massachusetts law books. There's a smaller fiction sec-
tion, and some local nature guides. I haven't
had a chance to go through everything. Why,
what is it?

*CONOR holds up a book and the camera zooms in on
the title:* Planning the Perfect Death.

MAGGIE

That sounds creepier than it is. I think it's
about setting up trusts and wills and that kind
of thing.

CONOR

Still a creepy title to fall given thousands
of options.

MAGGIE

Yeah . . . but at least we found it quickly, so
we know what the noise was. We can still get
some sleep.

*CONOR leaves the book on a nearby shelf, and
they turn off the light and close the door.
They cross the hallway. We cut again to the
outside-looking-in shot of the drawing room.
MAGGIE kisses CONOR and turns off the lamp.
We hear a gentle snore and then another thud,
followed by another. We repeat the sequence of
trudging to the library. The copy of* Planning
the Perfect Death *is again on the floor, several
feet in front of the doorway.*

CONOR

How did that fall again? I know I left it flat
on the empty shelf over here.

*Beside it is another book. When MAGGIE picks
the book up, the front cover falls off, and*

inside we see the title page for Unsettled:
Haunted Houses and Inns of Berkshire County.

                    CONOR
A little on the nose, don't you think?

                    MAGGIE
I've read it. This house isn't in it.

                    CONOR
Maybe it's auditioning for the next edition.

                    MAGGIE
I thought you didn't believe in ghosts?

                    CONOR
I don't. I just remember this scene in *Ghost-busters*.

*The library light is turned off again. We be-
gin a sped-up montage of the couple turning off
their light, hearing a book or two or three rain
down, going to check. The same two books are
found on the floor again, alongside others on
similar themes. CONOR eventually covers his head
with his pillow. MAGGIE puts in earplugs and
closes her eyes.*

                    MAGGIE
Maybe the house is trying to tell us something.

Nobody answers and we cut to commercial.

6

Cleaveland House was the coolest location we'd filmed so far, in my opinion, even if it was a full forty minutes from the motel. Stonemill Farm had its hidden orchard, and some of the others had been interesting enough, but this one was like a miniature castle. After the full crew meeting, in which we learned about the couple who had bought the house and the old woman who had died there, Felix caught my arm. He carried a heavy-looking black duffel in his other hand. "I need to talk to you about tomorrow night. This one is a big ask."

I didn't point out that he hadn't actually asked, just assumed it was in the job description: "other duties as assigned."

He escorted me past the day crew, about to start the tour, and into the house. I didn't have time to marvel at the beautiful entrance hall, but when he opened the door to the library I stopped to gawk. The door creaked as he pulled it shut behind us.

This library was like something out of a movie. It smelled like leather and pencil shavings and books. It was two stories tall: bigger than my town's basement library; bigger than my high school's library too. Most of the light in the room came from a large chandelier, though some bulbs were missing and others were dead. The shadows made the top corners darker, like the room stretched away forever. Some first-floor shelves had been emptied, but the upper ones were still full of ancient-looking leather covers packed shoulder to shoulder. A library ladder ran on a brass track around three sides of the room and part of the fourth, stopping when it got to the massive fireplace, so that you'd have to go most of the way around the room rather than jump that one gap.

The second floor (second floor!) had a narrow wrought-iron walkway around it, supported by iron pillars below, with a single waist-high wooden safety railing that looked like an afterthought. The balcony was interrupted by gaps for ladder access once on each of the two non-fireplace, non-window sides.

There was no furniture. I wanted it to have all the accoutrements a room like this should have: a leather couch, or perhaps velvet: tall reading chairs; a massive wooden desk with a lamp. A globe depicting countries that don't exist anymore, or countries that never existed. An atlas on a tall reading stand, open to a map with "Here There Be Dragons" writ across the ocean. Their absences made the room feel more intimate. A shrine to books, holding only books.

There were only two breaks in the floor-to-ceiling shelves. The top center shelves stopped short beneath a single round stained-glass window near the ceiling, which cast a single round of sapphire-tinted daylight on the bare hardwood floor. Opposite it, an ornately tiled fireplace. The interior of the fireplace depicted in relief a gaunt face surrounded by swirling hair.

"Nice touch, right?" Felix followed my gaze. I'd forgotten he was there.

"Is that what we're going with? Haunted fireplace?"

"Nah, done it before. I have something better in mind, with your help." He pointed upward. "What do you see?"

"A narrow-ass balcony that nobody with a fear of heights would set foot on."

"You, uh, aren't afraid of heights?"

"It's surmountable. I made it across the roof of the Victorian in town a few weeks ago. Deep breaths, et cetera."

"Okay, good. Now, what else do you see?"

I tried to figure out what he was going for. "The shelving goes all the way up except the window, and all the way around, except the fireplace."

"How do you know the shelves go all the way around?"

I realized what he meant. From where we were standing, just inside the door, I could see three sides of the room, but not what was above me. I was filling in the blanks with my own imagination. A few steps brought me into the center of the room, from where I could look at the second floor above where we'd been standing. It looked exactly like I'd expected; there had to be something else he wanted me to notice. Was there a door I didn't see? Something about the fireplace?

"I don't see—oh." I saw it. On the first floor, the bookcases went all the way around, with wedge-shaped shelves at the corners. The second floor had gaps in the corners on the fireplace wall, where the edges of the cases nearly met, but did not. The corners were dark enough that my mind had filled in those blanks as well.

"How big are the gaps?" I asked with trepidation.

"Funny you should ask. The bookcases are really deep because of the size of some of the books, so that one"—he pointed at the place where the fireplace wall met the wall on the side we'd come in—"is deep enough that once I squeezed my shoulders and ass in, much larger than yours, I might add, there was enough space to sit pretty comfortably. If we set it up so we're always hemming them in by filming them coming through the door, or in front of the creepy fireplace, they'll get used to not coming around to where you're standing now, and they'll never have an angle on you. And if we move the ladder to the other side after you're up there, they won't think someone walked all the way around."

"So I'm going to go up there and hide and then do what?"

"There are some amazing used bookstores in this area." He reached into his bag and pulled out a handful of books. I saw *Planning the Perfect Death, Ties That Bind,* a pharmacology primer, *Unsettled: Haunted Houses and Inns of Berkshire County.*

"Wait, is your story going to blame somebody for the old woman's death? The nurse? I'm not sure that's cool. And *Planning the Perfect Death* looks like it's about estate planning and living directives, not murder."

"I'm not picky. The couple can decide on their own storyline, with our push. Maybe the ghost is just upset the house didn't go to her cats or something."

"And I'm supposed to hide up there and then . . . ?"

"Chuck my books at the floor. I tested it earlier. They make a really good thump from up there. The sound bounces off the underside of the catwalk."

That sounded reasonable; too reasonable. I'd even be indoors for once. Given the apologetic way he'd approached me, he had to be leaving some crucial detail out. "So why did you call it a big ask?"

"Well, the thing is, the ladder needs oiling. The owners know it too, so I can't just grease it up, because if they try to move it again and it doesn't squeak, they'll know we were messing with it. And footsteps on the iron walkway echo pretty badly, and you heard how the door creaks too. So you have to get in place while they're filming outside tomorrow afternoon, and you can't leave until we get them out of the house the next morning. You can sit or stand, and when they aren't in the room you can walk around a little, quietly, but otherwise you're stuck. Ms. Tran says you can bring your phone, though, if you make absolutely sure it's on silent and you hide it whenever someone comes in."

I understood now why it was a big ask. "How do I eat? Or pee?"

He smiled uncomfortably, put his duffel on the floor, and reached into it again like Mary Poppins, handing me a black blanket, a box of protein bars, a water bottle, Gatorade, a warm iced coffee, a roll of toilet paper, a wet wipes packet, an empty ziplock, and a wide-mouthed Mason jar, ominously empty. That was the big ask. PA was a shitty job when it came down to it. I'd done some fun hauntings, and now I had to hide in a dark corner peeing in a bottle all night.

"I didn't have time to find one of those stand-up pee things for girls."

The closest I'd get to an apology. "This is a desecration of a beautiful library."

"It is," he agreed. "But you'll see, it'll be worth it if we get this right."

He met me the next afternoon while the couple and Jeremy filmed something in the backyard. He was anxious for me to get up there before the day crew returned—"so they don't look your way and give up the ghost, so to speak"—but gave me enough time to pee in the portable toilet on the lawn. I checked my phone for the millionth time: no messages from Jo, though I didn't remember giving her my number.

I entered the library through its creaky door and climbed the squeaky ladder, situated at the farthest point along the rail from my destined hiding place, then walked three sides of the reverberating balcony. Shimmying through the tiny slot that hid a slightly larger alcove, I doubted that Felix had managed to fit himself through; he'd seen the gap and sensed opportunity.

The first few hours weren't bad. It was still daylight, so I didn't have to worry about my phone's screen giving me up. I browsed the books I'd be tossing later. The door's squeal gave me enough time to hide when anyone came in, so I was able to leave my crevice for good chunks of time, even if just to stretch my legs at the balcony's corner.

I wasn't usually around for Jeremy's meet-the-buyers/meet-the-house set pieces, so it was fun to eavesdrop on the scene. I heard him suggest to the woman, Maggie, that she ride the library ladder like Belle; I tucked myself in and sat cross-legged, to make myself as small as possible in case her ride brought her to an angle where she might look up and see me.

I heard her explain how this was her dream house, and the library was her favorite part. That made me feel lousy about staging the scare here, though with a room like this, it was always going to be the focus for the episode: the most unusual feature was always the source of the haunting. Surely the owners knew too? Anybody who watched the show could figure that much out. If not, they'd just have to make peace with their "ghost" like the orchard bros had.

After they finished filming the library scene, I was faced with several hours of nothing. This time I had my phone to show me time's passage, not to mention the changing light through the high round window. I ate a protein bar and called it dinner. I leafed through another of the books I was supposed to drop, *Unsettled: Haunted Houses and Inns of Berkshire County*, hoping to find one of the houses we'd worked on. I didn't recognize any of them; I guess for our purposes, a known ghost was trickier to replicate than one we concocted.

The sun set and left me in darkness. I didn't mind. Like most of the houses I'd haunted, this one didn't scare me. The library was cozy, or it would be once it had furniture again. The air was still and warm, though it may not have been as stale at floor level as it was in my dusty cubbyhole.

I wouldn't have minded a nap—the long weekend had again confused my internal clock. I forced myself to stay up, straining to hear what was going on outside the library: the owners as they got ready for bed, Jeremy's cheery goodbye, the front door closing behind him, a low murmur that I was pretty sure was the crew explaining to the couple whatever they were going to film next.

I waited until the silence outside the room suggested they were in bed and settled, then waited some more. Always wait a little longer, I'd learned; the owners usually rewarded my patience with bigger reactions.

I started with *Planning the Perfect Death,* to set the mood. I leaned over to throw it as close to the door as possible, to make sure they saw it immediately when they walked in. It wasn't a huge book, but it was hardcover, and Felix was right that it made an excellent sound crashing to the floor. Then I retreated into my crevice to listen.

"Where's the light switch?" The camera silhouetted Maggie on the shelves opposite the door. Andi circled around to box the couple in, so they wouldn't think to step into the middle and look up, even though that would be the natural thing to do. They read the book's title, and the guy, Conor, freaked appropriately, before his wife tried to calm him down.

"That sounds creepier than it is," said Maggie. "I think it's about setting up trusts and wills and that kind of thing."

Score one for the librarian. Maybe she'd start imagining a friendly advisory ghost, telling them it was never too early to think about the future.

"Still a creepy title to fall given thousands of options."

"Yeah . . . but at least we found it quickly, so we know what the noise was. We can still get some sleep."

They turned off the light and shut the door again, leaving me in soft darkness, soft silence. This library felt safe, not scary. It made me root for Maggie the librarian's sensible approach. A skeptic always made the job a little harder, even if it made for good television to play them off each other. There had to be a sweet spot between skepticism and the vegans' terror.

I didn't want them to get too comfortable, so I picked a second book from my stack and flung it at the floor. *Unsettled: Haunted Houses and Inns of Berkshire County.* It made a satisfying smack, which was immediately followed by the distinct sound of a second book hitting the floor; I hadn't thrown two. Maybe they had left the first book haphazardly on a shelf, and mine's reverberation had somehow knocked it loose again.

Conor was the first through the door. "How did that fall again? I know I left it flat on the empty shelf over here."

The top of Andi's head came into view as she circled round.

"A little on the nose, don't you think?" Conor again; I guessed they'd looked at the title of the second book I'd thrown.

"I've read that book. This house isn't in it."

"Maybe it's auditioning for the next edition."

"I thought you didn't believe in ghosts?" asked Maggie. Ooh, that was good, if he had been the skeptic and they were switching roles.

"I don't. I just remember this scene in *Ghostbusters.*"

I almost laughed when Conor said that. Felix had been specific about not wanting to duplicate *Ghostbusters*, even though in his words, the scene in question was a master class in practical effects. "What I wouldn't do for a card catalogue and a fan," he'd said wistfully. Of course, nobody needed to be actually frightened during the movie's filming, so the noise of a fan wouldn't have spoiled the effect. So many techniques looked great on screen, like flying books through the rafters on wires, but those things wouldn't work when we had to convince the people in the room as well as the viewers. Movie magic and real-time magic were two different things, I'd learned.

The Fergusons and their entourage left the room again. I waited to make sure they didn't pop back in; some owners liked to try to gotcha their ghosts. If I gave it a few minutes, they'd settle into sleep and irritation (with the house, with the ghost, with each other) and exhaustion would begin to creep in.

Thunk.

Something heavy hit the floor below me. My hand automatically went to my book stack to make sure I hadn't accidentally knocked one over, even though my hiding place was far from the edge.

Thunk.

Another book fell, and this time I was sure I hadn't knocked it. Had Felix stationed someone else here with me without mentioning it? For some reason the thought creeped me out. I didn't mind being alone in the darkness, but I didn't like the idea of being alone in the darkness with someone else.

"Hello?" I whispered. "Is anybody there?"

Silence. Then another book falling from somewhere above my head, where nobody should have been able to reach, to the distant floor. Then another. I was about to investigate when the door creaked open, and I realized I'd almost exposed my hiding place. I stayed still as another heavy volume hit the ground.

The chandelier flickered to life. I scanned the balcony across from me, but didn't see anyone.

Conor picked up the book that had landed at his feet and read the title: *Massachusetts Pharmacy Law.* The others were law books as well. "There's got to be someone up there doing this."

"I can shine a light up there," said Andi. "So we can get a better look? Here."

Footsteps, and then a bright light trailed across the opposite side like fingertips searching for a title. I concentrated on making myself as small as possible and willed them to be too tired to actually venture up the ladder.

"Nobody's there, Conor." Maggie stood near the center now. If she stepped another foot back and looked up, she might see me. I pulled the visor of my black baseball cap low over my eyes, trying to minimize the white of my face.

"So, what," Conor said. "We have a litigious ghost? The old lady is trying to tell us something?"

"Maybe she's saying these books are outdated?" She sounded like she was trying to convince herself.

"I love it when you talk librarian. Do you think you can convince your ghost to let us get some sleep, since you've decoded her message to us?"

Maggie's laugh sounded forced.

They turned the light out and left again. I checked my phone: 3 A.M. It was probably safe to stop now to let them get a couple of hours' sleep before starting the day's work with Jeremy. I could doze in my corner and wait for Felix to tell me the coast was clear.

A book hit the door, as if it had been winged like a Frisbee.

"For fuck's sake," someone said from the hallway. It might have been Andi; whoever it was, that would be cut. This time, Maggie flipped on the light and marched straight to the ladder. I receded into my alcove, crouched low, like a gargoyle. If I lifted my head, she'd see me, so I had to count her steps to guess how close she was. After a moment, she said, "There's nobody up there," and descended.

I exhaled. Waited until everyone had left, waited longer. Whispered, "Whoever you are, knock it off. We're done for the night."

"If you say so," said Jo's voice, inches from my hiding place.

Of course. "What are you doing here?"

"Helping you."

"Why? Did Felix tell you to? I thought you were mad at me. How did you even get back here?"

"Do you care? You said it yourself, we're not friends."

"I still want to know if—" I didn't finish my sentence. I wasn't sure anymore why it mattered. She didn't say anything else, and didn't throw anything else, and eventually I balled my hoodie up like a sweatshirt and got a couple of hours' light sleep. The doorbell woke me at six. My instructions had been to sneak out the back door when Jeremy pulled the owners out front for their rise-and-shine interview.

It meant I was later than the rest of the night crew in leaving again, so I missed the morning meeting. It would've been nice to hear how it went from the perspective of somebody on the ground floor, but I didn't mind returning to the motel. The weekend had turned my sleep around again; I should've just stayed nocturnal.

The motel room smelled marginally better than it had the day I left, though you could still tell there had been a fire. The bedspreads reeked, and the curtains. Cath had clearly holed up for the weekend, sans hot plate; the small trash cans overflowed with takeaway containers. I tied up both bags and took them to the dumpster around back. Changed out of my work clothes, covered in dust from the corner where I'd spent the night, then collapsed into a long, dreamless sleep.

Got up in time for my afternoon swim, showered, headed over to the restaurant. The others were already there with drinks and food in front of them.

"We wondered where you were," said Ms. Tran.

"This is when we usually meet." I double-checked the time on my phone.

"We decided this morning to start half an hour earlier tonight."

"I was still stuck in the house when you met this morning. Nobody told me."

She shrugged. "You should have asked."

It struck me as deeply unreasonable. Everyone always went straight to bed after that meeting, then woke for this one. When was I supposed to have asked anyone? I was about to protest, to suggest someone text me next time; then I remembered how replaceable I was, and shut up. It wasn't any different from the teachers who expected you to ask a classmate to catch you up when you were absent, even if you didn't know anybody else in the class. Unfair, but nothing I could change.

Sathya ducked her head into our room to ask if I wanted anything, and I ordered a cold sandwich off the diner side of the menu, just to make sure I wouldn't cause more delays.

"I'm sorry," I said after she left. "What did I miss?"

"Jeremy's filming with us tonight," said Andi. "We're sending the couple to dinner at the Inn—that's why we're meeting early, to get some footage of them eating under the stars—and then Jeremy will 'randomly' bump into them and find a way to ask to meet their ghost."

"It'll give you a chance to reposition yourself," said Ms. Tran. "You'll want to park at the end of the driveway. I asked a couple of day crew folks to leave their vehicles and carpool to the motel for the night so yours won't stand out as the only one around when they arrive after dinner."

Felix wiped the corners of his mouth with his napkin, then leaned his chair back on two legs. "Maybe not so many book drops tonight? The rhythm was off. We needed them to settle in between getting drawn in again. We'll change it in edits, but there's no point in rushing it, yes?"

Here again, something I wanted to protest. It had been Jo's bad timing, not mine. I had known that in the moment. Was she getting the same reprimand? Nobody liked a snitch either way, so I just nodded.

It bothered me, though. On the way out of the restaurant, as we prepared to split—them to the Inn, me to the house to hide again—I stopped Felix. "I'm not really sure we need two of us in there. I was doing okay on my own."

"You did fine," he said. "Just a little overeager. But why do you say two?"

"The floater from day," I said. "Jo?"

He frowned. "Nobody told me they were sending anyone. Which one? Eagle? Irish Joe?"

I didn't know her last name. "I don't know. Eagle's a guy, right? One of the others. She's come by to help a couple of times now." I still wasn't willing to say she'd done the cow noises.

"Hmm. I'll try to find out. They're not supposed to interfere with what we do. And all of the Joes are union, so they shouldn't be doing double shifts anyway. If you see this person, say you've got it handled. You've done well so far, and I trust you to do this. Just don't go overboard and scare this couple away like you did in the pasture."

Maybe I should have blamed that on her; it wasn't like any of it was a lie. He shook his head, clearly thinking about the cows again, and left me to make my way to the house.

TRANSCRIPT
HAUNT SWEET HOME EPISODE 717—ACT IV

Shot of JEREMY outside Cleaveland House, balancing a cardboard carrier with three paper coffee cups on a box of donuts.

                    JEREMY
I can't wait to find out how the Fergusons' first
night in their new house went.

JEREMY knocks on the door. He's greeted by a hollow-eyed MAGGIE and CONOR, who step onto the porch, closing the door behind them.

                    JEREMY
Wow. You two look rough. Is everything okay?

                    CONOR
We didn't get a lot of sleep.

                    JEREMY
Oh, I'm sorry to hear that. I brought coffee,
if it'll help. Too excited?

                    MAGGIE
No. Somebody was culling the library all night.

                    JEREMY
Sorry?

                    CONOR
Falling books. Ghost.

                    JEREMY
Ghost?

                    MAGGIE
We think somebody who used to live here was a
librarian and she's trying to tell us to get
rid of the outdated books.

                    CONOR
That's Maggie's theory. I think it's the old
lady, the last owner, trying to tell us there's
some inheritance thing going on. Not like the
movie—something fishy about how the estate was
dealt with. Which would suck for us. I still
love this house, ghost and all.

                    JEREMY
Glad to hear it, because we have lots of work
to do. Have you decided where to start?

         CONOR   MAGGIE
         Kitchen.   Bathroom.

I think we're going to need more coffee.

*Cut to kitchen counter, eating donuts and drink-
ing coffee.*

                    CONOR
Okay, hear me out: the kitchen is the hub of the
house. I won't feel at home here until we have
a functional kitchen.

                    MAGGIE
But we do have a functional kitchen. It works,
it's just old. The fridge keeps things cool,
the stove makes things hot. So what if it's
ugly? Meanwhile, I'm not particularly comfortable showering al fresco, and it's going to get
cold sooner than later.

Plus, unlike the kitchen, we *like* antique fix-
tures in a bathroom, so it's just a matter of
cleaning and paint and grout. We don't need to

break it down or remodel or replace anything as
far as I can tell.

                    CONOR (sighing)
She's right. The kitchen can wait.

                    JEREMY (V.O.)
With our plan of attack finally decided, we got
ready to tackle the day's projects.

*Montage of CONOR and MAGGIE scrubbing the bath-
tub and the sink, CONOR and MAGGIE playing rock,
paper, scissors to decide who has to clean the
toilet (CONOR), JEREMY showing them various
paint colors for the walls. MAGGIE points to
bright white; CONOR points to taupe.*

*More sped-up footage of the bathroom makeover.
Eventually, all three go outside and collapse
in the grass.*

                    JEREMY
Obviously the paint needs to dry, but . . . who
gets the first shower in the brand-new bathroom?

          MAGGIE (firmly)   CONOR
          Conor.   Me.

                    JEREMY
I'm glad that's settled. In the meantime, what's
for dinner? I don't know about you two, but I'm
starving after all that work.

                    MAGGIE
Takeout, maybe? Or delivery, if anybody deliv-
ers out here? I'm too tired to cook.

                    CONOR
Me too.

                         JEREMY
If I may suggest, there's a great restaurant at
an inn a couple of towns over. Cozy, romantic.
Just the thing for a couple who just scrubbed a
decade of someone else's filth out of a bathroom
together.

                         MAGGIE
Sounds lovely. You're right about the paint,
though. I guess we're stuck using the outdoor
shower for one more night.

*Shot of CONOR heading resolutely toward the
outdoor shower with a towel and a toiletry
caddy. Cut to CONOR and MAGGIE sharing a bottle of wine and eating on a patio strung with
fairy lights.*

                         CONOR
This is lovely. I'm glad to know there are good
restaurants out here on the nights we're both
too tired to cook.

                         MAGGIE
It's perfect. We should toast to our new country life and the new old house.

                         CONOR
Yes, to the new old house. And to the ghost,
which doesn't exist.

                         MAGGIE
To the ghost, who totally exists, who will
hopefully let us get some sleep tonight.

They clink glasses and drink.

7

The day crew had mostly vacated by the time I got to the house, and nobody who was left looked my way.

Standing in the center of the library, I spent a moment absorbing the room's silent peace. Maybe we were jerks to choose this beautiful space for our haunting and make it less welcoming. That was the job, though, and the new owners had signed on for it.

I hauled Felix's second stack of tossing material up the ladder. Once it was safely in my alcove, I inspected the other corners. There was a matching cubby to mine on the other side of the fireplace, on the walkway's far end, but I didn't see any evidence that anyone had been in it. I'd practiced leave-no-trace haunting in my nook, carrying out my protein bar wrappers and drink bottles when I left, but my flashlight showed I'd disturbed a thick layer of dust. My questions of where Jo had hidden, and when she'd come in, remained. I was definitely alone now, though.

I sat on the balcony and read by the dwindling sunlight, then my phone's flashlight. Felix had left me a fine selection for this evening: a few mildewed inheritance law books with good heft, and *Ghosts of Berkshire County*, considerably slimmer. I wasn't sure what point a ghost would make by tossing copies of local paranormal books that left its own haunting out. Jealousy? Editorial comment? Felix's problem, not mine.

It was definitely the most interesting of the books at hand, so I paged through, examining pictures of Old Coot, haunting the ski slopes where he'd once had a cabin, and reading accounts of the phantom steam engine that had passed through Pittsfield "last year," inspiring the book. I flipped to the copyright page—1955.

Ghosts of Berkshire County was older than the haunting book from the night before by several decades, and much broader in scope, while *Unsettled* had concentrated on houses and inns. This one included sections on hospitals, ski slopes, factories, cemeteries, "any place to which a ghost or spirit might attach itself." I looked for the cemetery in the orchard, but it wasn't mentioned. Maybe lucky places were haunted; the rest were just forgotten.

Tires crunched on gravel, and I reluctantly wedged myself into my corner in case they visited the library first. One car, then the production van with its whiny brakes, then, a few minutes later, another car, then slamming doors. Fergusons, crew, Jeremy, followed by a pause, which I guessed was preparation for the shot where the couple would invite Jeremy in.

"So what's the plan for tonight?" Jo's voice from outside my alcove interrupted my listening.

"Same as last night, but hide, quick! They might come in any second and see you."

She shrugged. "I won't let them."

My annoyance from the other night returned. "Are you even supposed to be here? Felix said he doesn't know why someone from day would be floating across shifts, and he hadn't asked for any help."

"I told you, I'm here to help you, not him."

"That doesn't make any sense. I don't need any help. I'm doing fine on my own."

"Oh, yeah? What was your dying cow going to sound like?"

"I looked it up." My cheeks heated, which was a ridiculous response, like I needed to be embarrassed at never having hung out at a slaughterhouse. "I would have managed. Everybody says I'm doing a good job. I don't need you." Great. Now I sounded petulant.

"Nobody here cares about you at all. You're expendable. The only nonunion position. There's no upward mobility, no opportunity for a career, contrary to whatever your cousin might have told you, and he barely acknowledges you. Look at your roommate, exerting the only power she has by kicking you out every weekend. If any next-step position comes open, she'll get it, and you'll be trapped doing this until you quit or get fired. Don't you have any ambition to something greater at all?"

Her question stung more deeply than I'd expected, more when I realized the answer was no, I had no ambition at all. Hadn't I? I mean, I'd never known what I wanted to do with my life, but I'd thrown myself into this with enthusiasm. Hoped this might be the thing to stick. And yes, it was shitty hours for shitty pay, and yes, I was wedged into a dusty corner with an emergency pee jar and a protein-bar dinner, but hadn't it seemed at the beginning of the summer like Felix and Andi had taken me under wing? That maybe they'd been willing to show me how to do stuff, or to recommend me for a better job if something came along? I'd thought so, but now I wasn't sure, and I hadn't thought about it in weeks, with my weird upside-down schedule and omnipresent exhausted haze. How long had I felt like this?

Jo cut into my thoughts again. "Forget ambition. You're not even good at being you."

"I'm not sure I have any choice on that one." A bitter note crept into my voice, even as I tried to keep it light; I didn't want her to see that she was getting to me.

"Sure you do." She paused. "I can be you."

That wasn't what I'd expected her to say, and it caught me off guard. "I'm sorry?"

"Let me be you. Your family loves me. I know how to do this job, and I've got skills you don't have."

"And what am I supposed to do?"

"Be me, if you want, or be nobody at all. You're halfway there."

"My family would know the difference."

"Are you sure?" At that moment, she sounded exactly like me. Exactly like me as I sounded in my own head.

We had the same build, similar facial features. Not the same, but similar. Not that it mattered. "Who are you, Tom Ripley? You can't take over my life and expect nobody to notice."

"Maybe I'm joking, maybe I'm not. It's something to think about, anyway." She sounded like herself again. "So are we really repeating the book drop? Do we need to do one before they get here, or are we waiting until they've looked in once? They're almost to the door."

Her change in tone had me so confused I gave her a

direct answer. "If you heard them coming, we—I—should probably toss something quick."

"Yes, boss." Before I could throw *Intestate Succession*, she grabbed an armful of books from the second bookcase to my left, and flung them upward off the balcony.

"Not those," I hissed. The moonlight through the window caught them, and for one moment they were winged things before gravity took them to their flight's graceless end. A few loose pages fluttered down in their wake, still beautiful. "We're not supposed—"

"Ssh," Jo said.

The door opened. I ducked into my corner and crouched beneath my black blanket, trying to blend into the shadows.

Andi and Buzz raced through the door first—I knew it was them because Buzz slipped on one of the loose pages and swore in French, and Andi giggled.

"Oh, wow," Jeremy said. "So, is this what's been happening?"

I could hear the frown in Maggie's voice. "No, the other ones were just dropped flat. They weren't damaged."

"Didn't you call it a cull?" That was Conor. "What difference does it make if they land in one piece if the point is to throw them out?"

"It's our library, not hers! She can make suggestions, but I should get to decide which books stay or go. If she ruins them first, it's not much of a choice."

"Your ghost is a she?" asked Jeremy.

"I kind of just assumed. It felt right. She can correct me if I'm wrong. Ow!"

"Where did that come from?"

"It's called *Good Wives: Image and Reality in the Lives*

of Women in Northern New England, 1650–1750," said Conor.

I hadn't thrown it, which meant Jo must have.

"That's a good book," said Maggie. "It's not even that old. A really solid piece of scholarship. This can't be a culling suggestion."

"Maybe it's a clue to who she is," suggested Jeremy.

Conor said, "This house isn't anywhere near that old. I—hey!" The thud of another book colliding with a body.

"Maybe we should get out of here and come back when your ghost is less throw-y," said Jeremy. "My face is my money."

"She doesn't seem to be aiming at you," said Maggie.

My cousin must have found some courage somewhere, or found that argument persuasive. "Spirit, if you want to communicate with us, give us a sign."

Thud.

"Not that kind of sign," he said in a strangled voice. "I was thinking more like making the lights flicker. Can we cut? I need a medic. I think I'm bleeding."

Andi responded. "There's not even a scratch. I'm not going to stop filming for you to go get a bandage for nothing. This is good stuff."

"The union's going to hear about this," Jeremy said. "These are unsafe working conditions."

"Whatever." I could hear Andi's eye roll without being able to see her. "You work on a ghost show. Hazard of the job."

"What did she throw at him?" Conor asked after a moment. I took that to mean Andi had won the argument.

"*Three Men in a Boat*," Maggie said in a choked voice. "First edition."

"Do you get the feeling she's trying to hurt us, or communicate?"

A woman's voice bounced around the room, seemingly coming from all corners at once. "If I wanted to communicate with you, I'd just speak."

Dammit, Jo. That had not been anywhere in the plan. Maybe she was trying to get me fired, since she hadn't gotten whatever else she wanted from me.

"They must've hidden speakers," said Conor. "Wired up the room when we weren't here."

A cool idea, but as far as I knew, we had not done that.

"Do you guys want to take a break?" Jeremy asked. "We can come back later."

I didn't hear a response, but I guessed the crew rejected this plea like the last one. Jeremy's job was to keep them tense, not offer breaks.

"I want to see where the books are coming from," said Maggie.

"Do you think it's smart to go up there? What if it makes her throw even more?" TV Jeremy was trying to regain himself. Directing the flow of traffic while also trying to save his literal face.

"I'm gonna risk it."

"Beast, are you going to let your Beauty do this?" Oh, good, Jeremy, play the sexist card. I wondered if the line would make it through edits.

"She can do what she wants. My money is still on someone from your crew chucking books at us, which was more fun when they weren't valuable."

I was still hunched in my corner, but now I heard steps on the metal ladder across the room. Jo had to be hiding in the matching corner to mine, which meant if Maggie looked that way she would notice Jo.

"I don't see anything out of place," said Maggie. "Maybe on the other side?"

A voice spoke directly into my ear. "Uh-oh. She's going to find us any second."

Jo crouched behind me in my tiny corner, and there was no way she could have gotten behind me, no way at all. I screamed in surprise and leaped forward, misjudging the gap and slamming my right shoulder into the book-case. Someone else was screaming too, no, everyone was screaming, and books were sailing over the edge to crash on the floor below, and there was one louder scream rattling around the room, a dying cow reverberating through our bones. I still had my black blanket over my head, and struggled to get it untangled from my limbs. I thought I had farther to the railing, but then I was falling.

Jeremy broke my fall, the blanket softening the crash for both of us.

I lay sprawled on top of my cousin for a second before I caught my breath enough to check on him. "Are you okay?" I whispered.

"Mara? Is that you?"

"Yeah. Good to see you too." I tentatively moved a leg. Nothing seemed broken.

"What the fuck are you doing?"

"I'm okay, thanks for asking."

"I'm glad you're okay. Please get off me and tell me what just happened."

I got to my feet, gathering my blanket around me like armor. Off to one side, Andi checked on Maggie and Conor, their voices low and nervous. It was silly to bring this up now, but my mouth wouldn't stop. "Not before you tell me why you've barely said a word to me since I started here."

"What are you talking about? Sure, I didn't tell anyone we were related so you could do your job without anyone shouting nepotism, but I've dropped by your motel every weekend. Your roommate always says you're out, so I just figured you were having a good time and didn't want to hang out with me."

"You didn't say hi when I was up on the roof a few weeks ago."

"Mara, you were like fifty feet up. I don't even like thinking about heights and I thought I'd have to explain to my mother how I distracted you and you fell off. It wasn't time for a conversation."

"You never answer my DMs."

"My assistant runs my social media. You should have just text—"

"Is this somebody from your crew?" Conor interrupted, reaching out a hand like he was going to touch me to see if I was real. "I knew you guys were faking the haunting."

The room screamed again, a different tone, and I shook my head. "That's not me."

Another law book crashed at my feet, then another. The scream got louder and louder, pushing at us, displacing air, resonating with the room. Not a dying cow, but something else I couldn't name, just as insistent, just as mournful. It sucked all the air from the room, from our lungs. I gasped for air like a fish on land, and I heard the others doing the same.

One crystal shattered in the chandelier, then another,

and another, like microwave popcorn. We covered our faces, expecting a bigger explosion, but then the light and the sound went out at once, more like an implosion than an explosion, leaving utter silence and darkness in their wake.

After the silence came ragged breaths, and it was only when I heard the others that I realized I was breathing again too. I tried to regather myself.

They weren't supposed to have seen me. Weren't supposed to know I was there, though that didn't really matter anymore. I wanted out. I gathered my blanket around me and sprinted past my frowning crewmates, past the open-mouthed couple, past a confused-looking Jeremy, out of the library, and out of the house.

8

I crashed through the front door and down the dark driveway to where I'd parked, only to realize my keys were in my backpack, still wedged into my hiding place.

The car door unlocked itself and opened.

"Get in," Jo said, leaning over from the passenger seat.

I dropped to the ground next to the car, heaving from the fall and the run and the fright. "I'm not getting in there with you. What the fuck? How did you do that?"

"Doors don't really stop me."

"Yes, I can see that, but I don't just mean the door. Why are you being nice now when you nearly killed me five minutes ago?"

"I wasn't trying to kill you. Why did you jump?"

"I didn't mean to. I got tangled up and tripped when you scared me out of my mind sneaking in behind me. Anyway, you're saying that like you weren't being scary as anything in there. Threatening me, saying awful things . . ."

"Nothing untrue," she said sweetly. "Nothing you don't think about, even if you don't say it out loud. I stand by most of it. You should really get in, though. If someone from your crew notices you sitting beside your open car door they're going to think you've fallen and come over to help. No, wait, that would involve them noticing you."

"I give up," I said. "Are you just here to make me feel terrible about myself? To steal my job by making me run out on it? I don't understand."

"I think you do. For starters, you're still sitting there, and you're angry at me, and I scared you, but you're not scared *of* me. Get in the car. Come on."

It was true. There was something about her that seemed too familiar to be frightening. Reluctantly, I pushed to my feet and slid into the driver's seat. I sat there in the dark for a minute, eyes closed, still recovering.

"You're not a floater," I said at last. "Who are you? Do you actually work here?"

"My name is Johanna Bowen. And no, technically, I don't work for the production company. I'm here because of you, not them."

It was like searching for the missing piece of a jigsaw puzzle. "What do you mean, you're here because of me?"

"You're smarter than that. Figure it out."

"You first showed up at the cow haunting."

"I first introduced myself to you at the cow haunting," she corrected.

"So you were around before? Working? Helping?"

"Figuring myself out."

She fished in a backpack at her feet and I realized it was my own bag, which she must have brought from the library. She pulled out an apple wrapped in a brown paper napkin and offered it to me. It was a craft table apple, Fuji maybe, the kind my roommate swiped in bulk, waxed and shiny and remarkably unbruised despite having bumped around in my bag since whenever I'd put it in there.

Her fingers grazed mine as she handed me the apple, and electricity jolted me like I'd licked a battery.

I flung the apple over my shoulder. My car wasn't big enough for it to have far to go. It bounced off the back window and hit the tarp. The tarp. The sculpture.

"Can I have my keys, please?" I held out my hand, and she dropped the keychain into it, not touching me this time.

I started the car.

"Where are we going?" Jo asked. Johanna.

I didn't answer.

The nice thing about having stayed at the same home base for the whole summer was that I had started to know the area pretty well, at least in relation to the motel. The Fergusons' house was forty minutes north of the Mountainview, and Stonemill Farm was just west.

I parked down by the road, where Felix had told me to leave my car the night we dragged the fog machine into the orchard. The night I found a beautiful dead apple tree. It felt like years had passed since then, a hazy string of nights unconnected to days. It figured that working on this lousy basic-cable haunting show had roused my own personal haunting, a ghost who knew all the ways to make me feel worse about myself.

"No," said Jo. "You wouldn't."

"Why wouldn't I? All you do is tease me and push my buttons and try to outshine me at my own job." I groped by my knee for the lever to pop the hatch. A cool wind blew through the car as it opened; summer was almost over.

"I was trying to help!"

It had been a few days since I'd looked at my carving, and as usual, when I pulled off the tarp, I was shocked that I had made something this striking. It needed smoothing, polishing, time with tools I hadn't bought yet. It wouldn't win prizes for realism. It wasn't perfect.

None of which mattered. When I looked at it, I still thought: *I have made one special thing in this world. I have made one thing that speaks to who I am, and to who I want to be.* Even if nobody else could see that in it, I could. It made me proud.

"You can't do this," she said.

I wiped my eyes on my sleeve and slid my carving gently toward the hatch, tugging one corner of the tarp, then the other. I didn't turn. "You think I want to leave it here? The only cool thing I've ever made? I'd planned to keep working on it as long as I needed to, but how am I supposed to keep working on it, knowing you're going to keep trying to steal my life? And I'm not sure which is worse, that you're haunting me or that now I don't even know if I really made this, or if it was some weird orchard magic or something."

I didn't realize that was bothering me until I said it. Was any part of it my own, or was it just another thing over which I'd never had any control?

"The carving was all you," she said. "You caught a glimpse of me when you looked at the tree. I don't know how. Once you chose my tree, I would have found my way into whatever you made, whether it was a walking stick or a matchstick or a spoon. The real me; the old me. You putting so much of yourself into it that I got the combo meal was a weird bonus. I should have just been me, not me and you."

I used the bumper to lever it to the ground. Gathered the edges of the tarp and pulled. Way easier to pull than carry it, and a little gentler. Funny how I was still worried about damaging my carving, when I was about to leave it in the woods to rot, the way it was going to before I found it. Transformed it.

I reached the first of the tumbled gravestones.

"Please, stop," Jo said. "I was here for so long. I can't stand the thought of being here again. What if I disappear when you leave me? What if they decide they don't want an orchard and they cut it all down? Or one of those guys finds the carving and brings it to the house and I'm stuck with them forever? Arguing over bathrooms and selling small-batch artisanal cider and saying 'bro' every third word?"

"You weren't here for that filming."

"I was. I was already in the wood. And even if not, you were."

"You have my memories?"

She nodded. "You gave them to me. You put it all in the wood. Mara, you can't leave me here. You're not a cruel person."

"You keep saying 'I can't,' 'I won't,' like you know me. How do you know me so well when I don't even know myself that well? I'm so sick of not knowing. I have no idea what I want half the time. I feel like this unfinished lump of person. And see? I shouldn't be, but I'm still telling you everything. Why?"

She smiled sympathetically. "Because you know I understand. Part of you wants to drag your sculpture into the woods and bury it. Part of you is so proud of it you can't stand that thought, even if it means being stuck with me."

"Bury it?" My plan had been to leave it where I'd found it.

"Like I said, if the property owners find it, they'll be the ones stuck with me—but part of me is you, and you can't stand the thought of spending time in their company, which means some part of you is also reluctant to leave me to possibly get stuck with them."

True. "This makes my head hurt."

"I know. But ask yourself this: What happens to you if you leave part of yourself in the woods? Do you get those parts back, or are they just gone forever?"

The tarp snagged on something and I stooped to free it. It was caught on the broken-toothed grave marker, the one that read HAN.

"Han." Another piece clicked into place. "Johanna."

She nodded.

"How did you die?"

She frowned, thinking. "I should know that. It seems like an important thing to remember. Or maybe it's not important at all."

"What *do* you remember? About the real you?"

"Here," she said. "I think I can show you."

She reached over and took my hand. Again, a jolt; it felt like riding up the first hill of a roller coaster, full of potential energy. Then the air was rushing toward me, and I reached into the branches for an apple and dropped it in my basket. I was picking apples, October apples, even though it had been August a moment ago, and it had been night a moment ago, and the air was clean and crisp enough to bite straight through; the air tasted like apples, and bees were humming, and the ground was sticky underfoot.

We had six apple trees. Johanna. Johanna had six apple

trees, she and her two younger brothers and their father. Everyone said she was supposed to stay and continue looking after them, and she accepted it, even though her father wanted her to be married. She loved their farm, the cow, the apple trees, the workhorse, the way music carried through the trees.

And then I was on a stool beneath a cow, and she was flicking me with her tail, and I was telling her to stop, but in a laughing voice, like we had done this before, we had a thing going, a mutual agreement that she wouldn't kick my bucket and I wouldn't ever squeeze too hard. And then I was feeding scraps to the pigs, and hanging the wash between trees. And then I was a child dancing by the fire while my father played fiddle, filled with happiness; this was the whole world, and joy, and I was me as a child, dancing by the fire while my father played fiddle, the whole family in their enormous wooden chairs, and I was both of us, dancing, clapping, and I was thinking one day that will be me, I will be part of the music, I will have my chair, and then I was me, older, realizing I would never have my chair, recognizing my selfishness for wanting it, for wanting when it was unfair to ask it of my grandmother's twisting hands, that a chair or the lack thereof did not need to define me. How was I both of us? I still didn't understand.

Her mother's heart had given out in childbirth, and that same imperfection took Johanna at the same age, twenty-five, while she was collecting apples. She steadied herself on the tree she had just been picking from, then dropped to the ground without a sound, or with a small sound, it didn't matter, nobody was there to hear it. She saw herself from a bird's-eye view and the ground at once, the sky and the ground coming together. A widening, a heightening that smelled like dirt and rain and went on for the longest moment, a moment where she knew she had been ended, and she would never taste an apple again.

She was vapor, then vapor distilled. She felt a pouring-in and it was her pouring into a tree, and it was good, and time passed, and I felt my branches weighed down by unpicked fruit, overripe, rotting, spoiled. Feral, but not wild, a thing that needed help to get out of the place where I lingered in between states for so very, very long. Energy unchanneled.

Something changed: a path, a light, a path made of light, a knife against wood. An exchange. A loss; a finding. A funneling-through. Two selves poured into the same vessel to form a more complete whole. A commingling of old and new, dead and alive, complementary states.

She knew the ancient tree, had known it when it was young. Now the tree was dying, partially dead, cleaved, and she was not alone, there was someone else too, and she learned new things, things she shouldn't have been able to get her head around, but they poured into her and they were no longer unknown to her. Just like that, she was all of herself and all of someone else.

And who was the someone else? No explanation necessary. She was Johanna, but with everything I had poured into my sculpture. All of herself. Myself. Some alchemical copy. The carving should have just been mine—there was no reason for her to be there—but it was her tree I had chosen, the tree that had been the last thing she had touched, its apple the last thing she'd eaten. She had been nowhere and now she was here and she was herself and she was more than herself and what would *you* do with such an opportunity?

You would live.

You would do everything. You would try new words, you would play fiddle again and do this silly job, and how much easier it was when the rules didn't apply to you. She tested them all. She appeared and disappeared, made herself imperceptible, filled up a room with her essence then reduced herself to a spark. She could taste and smell things again. Play music. Make all the sounds she had ever heard. She could touch things, take what she needed, but she couldn't stray far from me or our carving, always drawn back as with an invisible rope.

The thing she could not do was be elsewhere. She was stuck with me, stuck with a frustrating person who was fighting her own nature, taking wrong turns, sabotaging herself. Jo understood. She'd binged the entire run of me, weeks ago, and now I'd binged the entire run of her, but also, for a moment, I'd seen me not as I saw myself, but as she saw me: free, open to possibility, full of life.

And then I was standing in the dark orchard, the dark cemetery, facing Jo again. She'd dropped my hand.

"Do you get it?" she asked.

I nodded, unable to speak.

What was it the book had said? "Any place to which a ghost or spirit might attach itself." The author hadn't considered that a ghost might become tied to something other than a location. Or that a ghost might not mind their situation. Nothing horrible had happened to her, and she had no debts to settle; she'd found a way to overflow a boundary unexpectedly imposed. Maybe that was what real ghosts did.

For Jo, my sculpture was the connective tissue, and I'd accidentally bound her not to it, but to me; or to both me and the carving? I had no concept of rules, only a rough map of the situation, a mental image of a mobile triangle, its angles constantly shifting as we moved in relation to each other.

A moment before, I'd pictured myself propping the statue up over the gravestone, a new monument. It wouldn't last as long as stone, and the stone hadn't lasted either. Now I knew I couldn't leave her here. She was annoying and probably bad for my career, but she didn't deserve to be trapped here, not the part that was her or the part that was me. I didn't know if I could leave her even if I tried.

Jo offered her hand, and I gave her two corners of the tarp. Returning to the car was faster than the outbound journey, and lifting it into the hatch was way easier with two people than one. We both stood looking at the sculpture.

"You couldn't have helped earlier? Or made your argument before I dragged this all the way out there?"

She shook her head. "You needed to see."

An SUV whooshed past, illuminating us briefly with its high beams before moving on.

"We should probably close the trunk," Jo said. "Otherwise, we really do look like we're dealing with a body."

I did as she said, closing the hatch and sliding into the driver's seat.

"I don't know what I'm supposed to do now," I said.

"Don't you?"

I thought about what I'd seen. The parts of Jo that were

me, and the parts that were her, and the things we had in common, even when we were not the same. She knew me as well as I knew me, perhaps better. I looked over at her; even her face was equal parts hers and mine. I could see that now as well.

"It'll take me a while to finish," I said. "And it might lose something in the transition."

"I believe in you. Anyway, we still have a few weeks of shooting. More houses to haunt."

I thought of my abrupt exit. "If I still have a job."

"Are you kidding?" She grinned. "Trust me. They loved it. You might get in a little trouble for going off script, but it'll make for great television."

TRANSCRIPT
HAUNT SWEET HOME EPISODE 717
FOLLOW-UP INTERVIEW

Drone footage follows JEREMY's car down a country road, then up a curved drive.

JEREMY (V.O.)
Two months later, I'm back to see how the Fergusons are doing with their haunted library.

JEREMY knocks on front door, is welcomed in by the smiling FERGUSONS.

JEREMY
Conor! Maggie! I can't wait to find out how you're doing.

CONOR
Come in and we'll show you around!

Cut to upstairs bathroom.

MAGGIE
We really haven't needed to do anything more to this bathroom since the work we did on the first day. It's functional and clean, which is a good start.

JEREMY
No more outdoor showers?

MAGGIE
No more outdoor showers.

CONOR

But we decided to leave it in place since it'll
be useful if we adopt a dog.

JEREMY

Oh, smart. How about the bedrooms?

*Cut to main bedroom. A before shot reminds au-
dience about the broken window and water damage, and the mattress on the floor that looked
like an animal had pulled stuffing out of it.
Sped-up footage of JEREMY and the couple tossing stuff out the window, cleaning, painting,
peeling up a corner of the carpet with trepidation. Dissolve to shot of new window, new off-
white paint on the walls. Hardwood floors where
the stained carpet had been. There's a wrought-
iron bed frame, the bed nicely appointed, and
two antique-looking dressers. There's a bedside
table on each side of the bed, the one on the
side closer to the wall covered in books.*

JEREMY

This looks terrific. I still can't get over this
gorgeous floor!

MAGGIE

We got so lucky. It's in great shape.

JEREMY

What about your kitchen?

*CONOR grins. Cut to kitchen. The camera sweeps
around the space. Another before and after. The
ceiling is still low, but the busy wallpaper
is gone, and the walls are a sunny yellow. The
appliances are all new, and the cupboards have
been replaced or refinished in light gray.*

JEREMY

Looking good!

                    CONOR
We still need to get to the ceiling and the
countertops, but getting rid of the wallpaper
went a long way to making it brighter in here.

                    MAGGIE
And he's in love with the new stove.

                    CONOR
Who wouldn't be? This is a kitchen I can cook
in. I can't wait to have people over for dinner.

                    JEREMY
You haven't yet?

                    CONOR
Well, there's the little matter of the dining
room table.

*Cut to dining room table, which is covered in
books in various states of repair, as well as
bookbinding paraphernalia.*

                    MAGGIE
It's been hard finding time to work on both the
house and the books, now that the semester has
started again.

                    JEREMY
I'm sure you'll get there, but that brings us
to the thing I've been dying to ask.

          MAGGIE   CONOR
          The library.   The ghost.

*Cut to the library. It looks bright and cheer-
ful, with daylight streaming in. There's a small
area rug, two comfortable-looking leather chairs,
a study carrel, a globe.*

JEREMY

Have you had any further contact with your ghost?

MAGGIE

Not since the night she threw things at us and chased your—

JEREMY

That was a scary night! You must be glad to have the place to yourself again.

CONOR

We can't decide if we want her to make contact again or not. I've gotten to like the idea. It was scary, but I never felt like the scary part leaked out of this room.

MAGGIE

And it's so nice in here during the day.

CONOR

It's like a puzzle I can't quite solve, who she was and what she wanted from us and if she left or she's just quiet.

MAGGIE

I was hoping maybe she'd make another appearance if I fixed up all the books she threw at us.

JEREMY

In that case, you definitely have a lot of projects ahead of you. Good luck with the house . . . and the haunting.

Credits roll.

JEREMY (V.O.)

Have you recently bought a fixer-upper that might be haunted? Apply to be on our show!

9

Jo was right about the Cleaveland House library. The haunting was edited to show my fall, the bursting chandelier, my swooping figure enveloping the host and then flapping out the door; the part where Jeremy swore at me by name, where I was revealed to be a person in a blanket, didn't make it to air.

The Fergusons' transition from cynical to believing played wonderfully. They had been sure the show was staged, or at least manipulated. My appearance, ironically, was what had convinced them: if the haunter was scared, the haunting must be legit.

We haunted a total of twenty-two houses, my ghost and I. On the weekends, I still camped and worked on my sculpture, with Jo for company. When the weather turned, Jeremy offered me the couch in his suite. Jo explored on those nights, within the generous range our weird triangle allowed, and on weekdays while I slept; she said we weren't going to survive the yoke (her word) if I didn't get some alone time, given that we didn't know how long we'd be tied together.

Jeremy was still too self-involved to give me much attention, but I did convince him to come with me to Lulu's for dinner once. He signed a photo of himself for the restaurant, and another for Sathya, who whisked it off for safekeeping, then returned to the table.

"I'm going to go to New York like you did," she whispered, handing him a mango lassi he hadn't ordered.

"Don't do it like I did," he said. "There are better ways."

When she'd left us alone, he took a sip of his gifted lassi and leaned in. "It's a myth, you know."

"What is?"

"The story that I got off the bus and immediately signed with a modeling agency."

"Didn't you shoot a jeans commercial the day your class graduated?"

"Have you ever seen it? I was a background dancer; I'm in like one frame. And then I did another forty-two auditions before I landed my contract—which is still success as those things go, but not a miracle. Editing isn't only for books and television, Mara. Tell your own story as you want it told."

I was still mulling that one over.

When the shoot wrapped, they offered me another season. I said I was no longer interested in cramming myself into cubbyholes, thank you very much; I'd gotten stitches twice, rabies and tetanus shots, and peed in more than my share of wide-mouthed jars. And still, I was bluffing. Despite everything, I had loved the job, and it was less isolated with Jo as a not-so-silent partner.

Ms. Tran called a week after I'd returned to Pennsylvania to offer me a job as assistant night production coordinator; my high-quality hauntings had elevated the game enough for them to create a new position. I said I'd consider it, then disconnected and walked back to the fire pit. It was mid-November, and most of the cousins weren't around, but my dad and his siblings were making enough noise to make up for it. Jo played along with "Springfield Mountain," by way of Woody Guthrie, which she said was similar to the version she grew up with, though the melody and lyrics differed slightly.

She stopped playing when I returned, and came over to sit in Jeremy's empty throne next to my own. The seat still needed shaping and smoothing, but that didn't matter; it was mine. It didn't even look out of place among the others, even if my skills were nowhere near Oma's yet. The first time I worked up the nerve to bring it home, on a long weekend in October, I took it to her first. She let out a low whistle and said, "Mara. What a thing."

I wasn't sure whether that was a compliment, but she ran her hands over it like it was a fine racehorse.

"The lines of the body are beautiful," she said at last. "And the not-quite-a-face is going to haunt me. Kid, when they say put yourself into your work, they don't mean put all of you into one piece. Bleeding for your art is fine, but it looks like you hit an artery. Is there any of you left?"

I nodded, wondering if she could see how complicated it actually was. I was still me; it was still me. It was Jo and it was both of us. Jo was still Jo, and me, and it.

Oma touched it again where the figure blended into the stump seat. "You know, you've done a better job than I did with the other thrones. This one is more you than any of theirs are them."

That surprised me. "You mean, you don't see shapes in the wood? What it wants to be? I always wondered when you asked me what I saw in a piece, and then you carved the thing I saw, if you were just doing what I wanted you to do."

"I would never!" She looked offended. "I know what's inside every piece of wood I work on—you see it too, I know. You always had a good eye. But I don't have any special insight into the intrinsic nature of anyone in the family; that would involve more people skills than I've ever had. They just believed me when I said what I saw. Who wouldn't want to think there was a lion or a dragon or a garden or stars inside them? No, those were fun, but yours is a much braver piece."

Everyone had stared as Jo and I carried it over to the fire pit one evening in October, but they shifted to make room. I caught them staring at me occasionally, and they gave me looks again when we dragged it to my car and took it with us at the end of the night, but nobody said anything to my face about it, either that night or now that we were crashing at Oma's for a few weeks.

Jo leaned over when I sat down. "What did Ms. Tran say?"

"She offered me something she was calling 'assistant night production coordinator.'"

"Which means?"

"The same stuff as before, only hiring someone else to do the parts that involve peeing in jars. A room of my own. Union."

"Are you going to take it?" She raised her eyebrows at me.

"Isn't the question 'are we'?"

"It could be fun. Maybe we'd get to suggest more ways to haunt things. I've been working on a new scream."

I considered. "And we definitely could do something else like the chandelier bursting."

She flopped back in Jeremy's chair and traced the arm. "Uh, this is probably a good time to tell you I didn't do that."

"What?"

"The chandelier, and the voice making it resonate, and the air-implosion thing. None of that was me. Cool trick, and maybe I can practice until I pick it up, but that was someone else. Something else. Definitely pissed off—I don't think it liked having me around. Why do you think I left so quickly?"

I replayed the night in the library in my head, trying to separate what I'd done from what Jo had done, and isolate what was left. If I could believe in one tree-chair-carving ghost, I guess I could believe in more.

The music picked up again and I sat back to listen. The sculpture felt comfortable wrapped around me. It was weird looking, maybe, intense for a chair, but it was mine, and it was Jo, and together we were going forward as something new and undefined. I grabbed a thick pine splinter from the kindling pile and started looking for a shape to release from the wood.

Acknowledgments

Books, like trees, have seeds and roots.

There's a sculpture at the American Visionary Art Museum in Baltimore that was carved from an apple tree. The Applewood Figure was made by a patient in a sanitarium, credited anonymously. It's his only known piece: a self-portrait with a hollowed-out chest to mark his tuberculosis and a rudimentary face that somehow conveys more emotion than a photograph. It's part of the permanent collection, and every time I go to the museum I spend a half hour communing with it.

When the World Fantasy Convention came to Baltimore in 2018, I sent a lot of people to that museum, and I remember that when I chatted with Jeffrey Ford after his visit, he mentioned the same carving. "I've always thought there's a story somewhere in there," I said. "Race ya," Jeff replied. I don't actually know who won, but I will thank Jeff here for invoking my competitive spirit.

The museum has added some other wooden pieces since then that also went into the DNA of Mara's grandmother's work—the names of the artists are mentioned in the story—so I will give further specific thanks to the American Visionary Art Museum. I never leave that place without new thoughts and ideas provoked by their exhibits.

The reality show in this book appeared under a different name in my novel *We Are Satellites*. Sometime after that book came out, I mentioned to some friends that if I knew how to pitch a TV show I thought this one had potential. "Or you can just write a book about it," said Neil Ottenstein. So I did! Thanks, Neil.

Early in COVID, J.R. Dawson and I had an idea to do online movie script readings for an audience of nobody. We've been doing them more or less monthly ever since, with Sean Nixon randomizing parts and a rotating cast of dozens of wonderful humans, some of whom you may know. I've learned more than I ever knew about scripts from this project, and I might even brave a full one myself someday, but this scratched some of that itch. Thank you, Zoom players who do not ever present, for so many entertaining nights.

My editors, Ellen Datlow and Eli Goldman, have shepherded this book through the publication process with joy, enthusiasm, and insight, all of which I greatly appreciate.

My agent, Kim-Mei Kirtland, also deserves copious thanks for her editorial acumen, clearheaded advice, humor, and conversation.

My gratitude to the whole team at TDC, including art director Christine Foltzer, cover designer Esther S. Kim, marketer Jordan Hanley, publicist Laura Etzkorn, social media star Samantha Friedlander, managing editor Lauren Hougen, production editor Dakota Griffin, copyeditor Sara Thwaite, proofreader Jaime Herbeck, and interior designer Greg Collins.

Aliza Greenblatt read drafts of this story, as did my

mother and sisters, and the Sparkleponies read portions of it at times that couldn't possibly have been convenient for anyone. While my father didn't read this early, he always asks interesting questions that roll around in my brain when I'm looking for stories.

My students and colleagues at Goucher and other far-flung places make me think about writing and process in ways that are good for my own writing and process.

Baltimore is full of amazing indie bookstores, including Greedy Reads, Snug Books, the Ivy Bookshop, Bird in Hand Coffee & Books, Atomic Books, and Charm City Books, and I'm grateful for their support and their inspiration in the form of books and events. . . . Between that great list and the museum I talked up above, you're ready to move here, right?

Thank you to you for reading this weird little haunting.

Last on the list but not ever least, I thank Zu, with more love and appreciation than she will ever know, even though I say it an awful lot.

About the Author

Karen Osborne

SARAH PINSKER is the Hugo, Nebula, and Philip K. Dick Award–winning author of *A Song for a New Day*, *We Are Satellites*, *Sooner or Later Everything Falls Into the Sea*, *Lost Places*, and more than sixty works of short fiction. Her stories have appeared in *Asimov's Science Fiction*, *Strange Horizons*, *The Magazine of Fantasy & Science Fiction*, and *Uncanny*, and in numerous anthologies and year's bests. She is also a singer-songwriter with four albums on various independent labels. She lives in Baltimore, Maryland, with her wife and two weird dogs. Find her online at sarahpinsker.com.